# Alternative Ed

*Alyce Shirleydaughter*

Note: This is the adult version
of the novella *Yo! Eddie!*
by the same author.

Published by Luminary Media Group,
an imprint of Pine Orchard, Inc.
www.pineorchard.com

Printed in Canada.

Additional information:
www.alyceshirleydaughter.com
www.louannejohnson.com

ISBN-10 1-930580-86-x
ISBN-13 978-1930580-86-2
Library of Congress Control Number 2007940392

2nd Printing—2008

# DEDICATION

*for Corey*
*who never meant to kick that teacher*

*and*

*for all the "secret readers"*
*who are sitting in school*
*keeping their intelligence to themselves*

# Chapter 1

I seen Miss Beecher today at the library checking out a old lady's book. She had her head tipped down so I couldn't see her face real good but I knew it was Beecher on account of her hair is the exact same color as a car I stole once. Bronze metallic. Beecher doesn't look like a regular librarian but she at least didn't look like she was falling off a cliff the way she did most of the time back when she was trying to be a teacher.

I didn't go all the way inside the library, just stood in the doorway waiting for Letty and the boys to finish listening to the story lady, but Juanito saw me and he yelled, "Eddie!" I quick looked at Beecher to see if she heard Juanito holler my name because if Beecher looked at me, then I would nod, maybe say, "Hey, how's it going." But she was busy helping another old lady find her library card so I ducked out.

First time I saw Beecher, I thought, oh great another one of those Peace Corps people with their organic shoes and their tofu sandwiches and their posters showing how important it is to save the whales and the rain forests and the baby seals and me and all the other semi-literate at-risk underprivileged economically deprived youth at the alt school who don't really give a shit about getting an education because what difference would it make if we did. We'd still be us. We'd still be freaks and losers except we'd be freaks and losers with educations, so we'd understand exactly what we couldn't have.

The day Beecher showed up at our English class, Edgar Martinez asked how long had she been a teacher. We knew Beecher was virgin the second she started to answer the question because the old teachers know better than to leave themselves open like that. Beecher told us she was going through a program for alternative certification because she didn't decide to become a teacher until after she already graduated college. So she said we had something in common because she was an alternative teacher and we were alternative students. For like two seconds, I started to fall for that idea, but I caught myself in time.

I don't miss Beecher or nothing, but at least she was better than the guy we have now who is a total pathetic pussy who wears pink glasses. He thinks if he tells us four hundred times a day that he went to Stanford University, then we'll appreciate what a big sacrifice he's making to be a teacher who gets paid crap and works in a place that looks worser than Juarez. He thinks we'll like him for devoting his life to helping disadvantaged kids become successful productive members of society but we mostly think he's a *pinche* dickhead. At least if he was driving around in a cool car with a hot stereo and a shiny rich girl in the jump seat, we could be jealous and hate him and maybe we would jack him up and take his car, but now we hate him worse because he could have had all that stuff and he was too stupid to take it so now nobody has it. If he really wanted to help kids who didn't have his advantages, he could of saved up his giant allowance and got his parents to buy him a real expensive car and then he could of just came here and gave us the money and the car. He could of even sold lottery tickets. I bet a lot of kids would go to school if they might win twenty bucks or a car just for showing up. But he blew it. How can you respect a teacher who wasn't even smart enough to figure that out?

Beecher didn't try to pretend she didn't appreciate her nice easy white girl life. And she wasn't scared of us like most of the lady teachers are, even though she's skinny enough that you could probably pick her up and throw her down the stairs real easy. And she didn't try to feed us all that crap about how useful our education was going to be someday, like how we would need algebra to figure out how many square feet of carpet we need in our living room because everybody knows that we'll be renting some crappy apartment our whole life and even if we could buy a house, measuring the carpet is the carpet guy's job and he probably has a calculator.

The first day, when nobody would open their grammar books to the page number she wrote on the board, Beecher didn't even yell. She just sat down on the edge of her desk, still holding her book, and looked around the room. Not with mean eyes. More like she was surprised that we weren't all following her. Like if a mother duck turned around and instead of waddling along in that nice neat little line, the baby ducks were running all over the place where they could get lost or killed so easy.

"Wouldn't it make more sense to exert a little effort and get through this material quickly, so we can move on to something more interesting and relevant to your lives?" Beecher asked us.

"Oh, yeah. Hah!" T.J. Ritchie laughed his hard dirty laugh. "Like how to sell more crack?" Ritchie is big, really big, probably seven feet tall, and he doesn't give a shit about anything. Usually new teachers give Ritchie that look that says you're a stupid-nothing loser and some day you'll be sorry you wasted your pitiful little life. Or they send him to the office or else just ignore him, but Beecher hooked her hair behind her ear with her finger like she does when she's thinking and said, "You're a drug dealer?"

Ritchie shook his head and made check-her-out faces at his friends and they were all like "Duh." Beecher walked over and opened the door. "Then you might as well go." She flung her arm out into the hallway.

"You can't kick me out," Ritchie said. "I didn't do nothing."

"I'm not kicking you out," Beecher said. "I want you to stay. But if you want to be a criminal, I can't help you."

"I don't need your help, lady. You think you're all better than us but you're not."

"I absolutely do not believe I am a better than you." Beecher shook her head and her hair sort of shimmered around her ears. "I can understand perfectly well how a person might decide to reject capitalism and corporate corruption and choose a criminal career over a traditional education."

By this time, Ritchie and everybody else was just staring at Beecher like she needed to get real, but she kept on talking. Her voice is thick and smooth like a talk show lady and she has this way of saying stuff that sticks in your brain afterwards and plays back even when you aren't thinking about it, like those TV commercials that get stuck in your head and drive you *loco*.

"You and I have different ethics and values, Mr. Ritchie," Beecher said. "I choose to live within the law because I could never survive being incarcerated, but if you don't mind risking your freedom in pursuit of a life that offers you fulfillment, that is your choice. However, analyzing literature will not help you be a more successful drug dealer which is why I suggest that if you seriously wish to pursue that avenue, you focus your efforts on your criminal career. The sooner you start, the better chance you have of being successful—until you are incarcerated or killed."

Ritchie didn't say anything for a minute and he probably would have let it slide except this one girl giggled, so he had to say, "Whatever." Then I think Beecher realized you should never talk that long to a kid like Ritchie because she closed the door real quiet and folded her arms and looked around at the rest of us.

"That goes for everybody," she said. "If you truly didn't want to be here, you wouldn't be. And I am not foolish enough to think I can make you do anything. So we won't even pretend that you have to do the assignments. And I would prefer not to have this discussion again."

We didn't have that discussion again, but we had a lot of other ones that the school board wouldn't have liked, even though they are usually pretty desperate for teachers because New Mexico is like 49 out of 50 when it comes to how dumb and fucked up the students are and how backwards the school board is and how fast the teachers give up and go away. If we lived in one of those smart states like New York or California, there would probably be a whole lot of teachers like Beecher, and she wouldn't even have to worry about getting fired for being a liberal intellectual.

One thing about Beecher I remember the most is that she would look you right in the eye when she was talking to you and you could tell she wasn't thinking bad things about you, even if you just said something real stupid or pronounced a word wrong when you were reading out loud. Like if you were reading something about trains and you said "dee pot" instead of "dee poe," she wouldn't let anybody laugh at you. She would just wait until you were done reading and then she would say, "Has anybody ever been to a train depot?" and she would pronounce it the right way to let you know how you were supposed to say it. The other teachers would jump right on that wrong word and pronounce it the right way the second you said it wrong because, even though they went to college and we didn't, they always have to show how smart they are. But Beecher was too busy trying to show us how smart we were instead of how smart she was, so by the time we wised up to how smart she was, she was already gone.

# Chapter 2

At Bright Horizons, it's pretty easy to get rid of a teacher. All you got to do is get a few kids to pretend the teacher inspired you to turn over a new leaf and live up to your potential and appreciate the opportunity to get a free education. That teacher will get so psyched about being your mentor and role model that they'll answer any questions you ask them, even if you slip in a question about evolution or gay marriage. Then you pretend like you just love going to school because you're learning so much and you talk about your cool teacher at home and all the parents get so excited they look like they're going to pass out. Then you repeat what the teacher said about evolution or gays in front of the right kid's parents—like those Anglos who have those little blue and white signs with the Ten Commandments sticking up in their front yard and—Boom! that teacher is history.

We didn't even have to pretend we liked Beecher to get her to say stuff she could get fired for. Like when Joey Dinwiddie said he and his girl were going to get married, Beecher said, "I bet you think if you get married, you'll be able to have sex every day." Joey laid back in his chair and puffed up his chest. "Damn right," he said with his big talking-about-pussy grin.

"I hate to disappoint you," Beecher said, "but getting married is the best way to make sure you don't have sex every day. If you don't believe me, go home and ask your father."

Everybody started making kissing noises and shouting out stuff about sex and a bunch of kids stood up and did some air humping. Beecher held up her hands and said, "You children obviously are not mature enough to be sexually active. If your only goal when you have sex is to experience an orgasm, then you are masturbating on other people. You would do better to have sex with yourself. No danger of disease, no possible pregnancy — and no broken hearts."

Kids started screaming their heads off as soon as Beecher said "masturbate." Beecher didn't even blush. She just waited until the screaming died down. Then she said, "My point exactly. If you cannot say the words *penis*, *vagina*, *breast*, *orgasm* and *masturbation* without giggling and blushing, then you are not mature enough to have sex."

Somebody ratted out Beecher for telling us to masturbate. Teeny White who works as a student clerk in the office said she saw Beecher go into Mrs. Nichols' office and Teeny could hear Nichols hollering and, when Beecher came out, it looked like she was crying. But there's so many pregnant girls in our school that they can't fire anybody for talking about sex because then it would get in the papers and the parents in this town freak out totally if they even see the words *sex* and *school* on the same page.

Mrs. Nichols visited our class the next day and sat in the back and wrote a bunch of notes and we figured Beecher was history but nothing happened. We couldn't figure it. Beecher isn't local, so she couldn't have cousins on the school board and nobody in her family is a county commissioner. Usually it only takes a month to get rid of a new teacher. Two minutes is our all-time record. But if they make it to the end of the first quarter, they usually last a whole year.

Beecher was still going strong by Halloween and we started to think she might make it, but then she read us this story the day before Halloween. It was just one of those dumb ghost stories that are supposed to be spooky and scary but only little kids are scared of them. Beecher lit candles and turned out the lights and put on some weird spaced-out music. It was actually pretty interesting and everybody was kind of getting into it, but about halfway through the story, Beecher read the word "damn" or "hell" or something like that. Nothing, really. Not even a real swear word. But this is Rosablanca, so when we came back to school the next day, T.J. Ritchie's mom ran screaming into the principal's office and said Beecher was preaching Satanism and Ritchie had been traumatized by the experience.

I heard it all because me and Jaime Sanchez were outside the main entrance trying to jack the change out of the pay phone. I seen Beecher going into Mrs. Nichols' office and then the bell rang for first period and we went to class and everybody was psyched because we didn't have a teacher. Then this counselor showed up and took roll and started talking about how much more money we'd make in our life if we graduated from high school instead of dropping out. I wondered what that counselor would say if I told him that T.J. Ritchie already makes a lot more money than he does and Ritchie don't pay no taxes on it, neither.

Beecher showed up about ten minutes before the bell rang, but she didn't say anything, just collected all her stuff. Her eyes were all red from crying. The counselor smiled real cheesy at Beecher and ducked out, and we just sat there so quiet I could hear the clock above the door that only has a minute hand and stutters just like Jerome Harding. *T-tick t-tick t-tick*. The ticking made me think about when Beecher said the most important thing she could teach us was to choose how to spend our time because your time is your life.

After Beecher had gathered up her stuff and walked over to the door, she turned around and opened her mouth partways like she was going to say something. I thought maybe she was going to say it was no big deal and she would see us in the morning, but she didn't. She just hooked her hair behind her ears with her fingers and looked at us all . . . one kid at a time. I thought she might skip over T.J. Ritchie, but she didn't. She looked at him exactly as long as she looked at me and her face didn't change. I thought she would of changed her face a little bit when she looked at me.

Nobody said anything, not even the kiss-ass girls. I almost said something. I almost said, *"Hasta luego,"* but I didn't because one little thing like that is enough to make a teacher think you care whether they live or die. If they think you give one little shit about them, they start working on you, trying to wear you down. "Tell me your story," they say, "I want to help you but I can't help you if you don't let me. Just tell me the truth." They think they want to know the truth. They think they can handle it.

But they can't even handle the easy shit, like how come Joey Dinwiddie's brother got straight A's and a full ride to some college out in Oklahoma where they promised him he'd be the starting quarterback but he sat on the bench for two years with the only other black kid on the team and watched dumb white farmers fumble every play until he got disgusted and came home. He didn't waste his education or anything. He got a job coaching at the regular high school.

But if a really smart kid like Dinwiddie couldn't make it, then what kind of chance is there for us regular everyday losers? None of the teachers ever has a good answer to the Dinwiddie question because there isn't one. That's just the way it is. Beecher might have thought of something. But by the time she showed up, Joey was tired of telling that story and the rest of us were tired of hearing it.

Every once in a while, when a teacher is too dense to get the message that they aren't really here to teach, they're just here to fill in the roll sheets so the alt school won't lose its funding and the regular school won't have to deal with us, Denny Clodfelter pretends like he's real interested in reading the stupid stories in our literature book. He even volunteers to read out loud which just about makes the English teacher pee her pants. Then, after the teacher gets all excited about finding a punk who appreciates literature, Denny will stop reading one day right in the middle of some story and he'll say, "You know, after your dad breaks a two-by-four across your face and you have to go around for the rest of your life looking like a flat-faced heifer, you just can't care about reading these stories. Like you can't get excited about some idiot who sells his fancy watch to buy some hair combs for his wife except she sold her hair to buy him a chain for his watch. Besides, that whole story is just bogus because who would want to buy some old used hair anyway?"

I bet somebody would buy Beecher's hair, though, even if it was used because it's so shiny like it has a million candles lit inside it. When she was standing in the doorway, trying to feel some kind of goodbye from us, I thought about giving her my journal that I never turned in after she asked us to write one important thing from our life. I wrote like six pages about how it feels to be a eight-year-old kid who idolizes his older cousin so much and how exciting it was when he finally let me ride with him one night and what a thrill it was to drink a cold *cerveza* and smoke a Marlboro with my arm leaning out the window of that car with the killer speakers and chrome spinners. And how it felt to watch *mi primo* get out of the car and leave the engine running and walk up and knock on this kid's door and then blow the kid's face off the second he opened the door and how I shit my pants and sat in it all the way home, smelling the stink of hopelessness that hung around my life.

I didn't give Beecher my journal, though. I figured she already had enough stuff to make her feel bad. Now she'll probably go teach some Indian kids on a reservation in Arizona like she used to talk about sometimes. It'll probably be easier out there. I don't think they have so much gangs and stuff because they got tribes and drums and sweat lodges. We learned about all that during Native American Heritage Week. Beecher brought in all these Indian stories, but she knew we never read our homework so she read us this one story out loud. It was written by this guy named Alexie who is a real Indian, and it was a pretty long story but it wasn't even boring. It was pretty sad, though, and I know Beecher read it to us because then we would see that our life isn't so bad because at least we got indoor plumbing and floors instead of just dirt, and the government doesn't try to take away our language anymore.

Maybe those Indian kids will appreciate Beecher. Maybe they'll like having a teacher that calls up their parents and comes to their house to shake their hands and sit on their falling-apart furniture to show how much she cares. Maybe those kids won't break the windows in her car while she's inside their house. They might even like her after a while. But we don't like that kind of teacher here. We don't need people feeling sorry for us. We need those hard teachers, the ones who know what it feels like to wake up hungry every day for sixteen years. The ones who catch you all by yourself in the hallway and grab your shirt and slam you up against the wall and say, "You're such a fucking loser" and then just drop their hands and shake their heads and walk away. Those kinds of teachers might be able to handle the truth if I ever felt like telling them, but I doubt if I ever will. What difference would it make if I did?

# Chapter 3

Today in school this new kid from Ohio said people in New Mexico are lazy because everybody on his street parks their car right up in their yard near the front door where you would have some nice grass if you lived in one of those green places.

"I don't see why they can't even walk a couple steps to their door," the stupid Ohio kid said and I was going to explain that his neighbors might be lazy but probably that isn't why they park in their yard because if they don't got a handicap ramp and they park right in front of their door, then they could be a dealer or some kind of gangster who doesn't want to get shot trying to get from his house to his car or vice versa. But I didn't tell him because Henry Dominguez already told him to shut up and go back where he came from if he didn't like it here.

The Ohio kid's ears got all red and I felt kind of sorry for him because I don't know how many times somebody told me to go back where I came from except I am where I came from and they're too stupid to know it—even though everybody has to take American history and it's right there in the book that a whole bunch of states used to be Mexico, like Texas and New Mexico and Arizona. Like *mi abuelo* always says, "We didn't cross the border, M'ijo. The border crossed us. The Corazons been living here for 300 years."

When Miss Beecher was here, we used to have some pretty good class discussions about stuff because Beecher was like one of those little sheep dogs that you see on the Discovery channel where they don't make any noise, but they keep all the sheeps going in the right direction and if one of the sheeps starts getting any big ideas and gets out of line, the little dog just bites it on the butt. But our new *pinche* dickhead teacher Mr. McElroy believes in democracy and it doesn't work any better in our English class than it does in our government because only the real big guys get free speech and everybody else knows if they say what they really think, who's going to be waiting to whack them after class. McElroy tried to start a discussion about the border controversy after Henry told the Ohio kid to go back where he came from and the Ohio kid told Henry to go back where he came from, but as soon as McElroy asked for comments, T.J. Richie laid back in his chair and said why don't we let those Minute Men who bring all their guns and sit on the border in their lawn chairs just get up off their asses and do what everybody knows they want to do.

"If we just let those Border Patrol wannabes shoot the stupid Mexicans, then we wouldn't have a border problem," T.J. said. He doesn't give a shit about the border, but he likes to get things started.

"That would be murder, you stupid ass," said Teeny White whose mother is Mexican.

"Those Minute Men guys are the ones who are stupid," T.J. said. "I mean, I'm white and everything—"

"You sure about that?" Henry Dominguez hollered and the tortilla crowd cheered. But T.J. Ritchie doesn't care if you say shit about him being white because he's always saying there are two kinds of white people and he thinks he's one of the good kind because his mother drags him to church all the time and he knows a whole bunch of quotations from the Bible. They're mostly quotations about why it's okay to hate other people like gays or Arabs, but if anybody reminds T.J. that Jesus didn't hate people, he just says, "Oh, yeah? I'll pray for you to stop being so stupid next time I go to church."

"Those Minute Men are mostly those big fat dumb white boys who like to drive around the desert chasing down antelope and shooting them from inside their pickups," T.J. said. "They call that hunting. Effing assholes."

Then a bunch of other white boys who cut school every year during hunting season said maybe they should have open season on idiots like T.J., and McElroy blew his whistle and gave us a spelling quiz. I kind of wished that McElroy knew how to have a discussion because I had an idea when everybody was yelling. I was thinking what would happen if Canada decided they wanted to have more land, just like the Americans did back when they invaded Mexico. I looked it up on the Internet. In our history book, it says the "Mexican-American War" but in the Mexico history books it says the "United States Invasion of Mexico." Anyway, so the Canadians just decided to take Wisconsin and Minnesota and some of those other cold states up there where all the lakes are. And they had to kick some butt and kill a bunch of people, but they won and then they put up this big fence and said, "Now this is Canada and you can't come here and live or work unless we say so." And some people would say, "But our family has lived here for three generations." Or they would say, "My grandmother lives over there and I always visit her on weekends." But Canada would say, "Tough shit. Handle it. And you can't come here and work anymore, either, unless we say so. Even if you already worked here for years." And Americans would say, "How come you're acting so shitty instead of trying to get along with your neighbors?" But Canada wouldn't have to answer that question because they already got what they wanted. And Americans would just keep on sneaking over the border because they would feel like nobody has the right to split up families or just take somebody's land and say it's another country and then Canada would get real pissed and say, "Okay, we're making French the official language. How do you like them *mansanas*?" But probably if you tried to ask some Americans to think about my Canadian idea, they would just look at you weird and tell you to go back where you came from.

Anyway, all I'm saying is you should drive around the neighborhood at night and see if there are any cars parked in the yard right up by the front door before you buy a house in New Mexico. But if some new family is too stupid to figure that out then they'll just end up freaking out and moving anyway so it works out the same in the end.

# Chapter 4

People shouldn't be allowed to go around telling little kids to "Just Say No to Drugs" because that could be dangerous. Besides, "Just Say No" has to be one of the lamest ideas ever invented in the first place and I bet it was invented by somebody white who never had to sleep in the same bed with four other people who hardly don't ever take a shower because there wasn't any place else to sleep. Besides, if just saying no worked, then people would go around just saying no to stuff they didn't want to do anymore. Papi could just say no to being poor and unemployed. People would just say no to cigarettes and they wouldn't have to pay all that money to get hypnotized into quitting smoking. And all those white girls wouldn't be puking up French fries in the bathroom behind the cafeteria. And Bobby Chavez wouldn't be dead. Bobby said no. Except he said no to the wrong guys and they popped him just like that. And then they put it in the paper that it was a drug deal gone bad, all insinuating that Bobby was buying drugs, which was the first thing that came to most people's mind anyway because he was poor and brown.

It didn't matter that Bobby was president of the Spanish Club and the best player on the soccer team and made the honor roll every single time. They forgot all that stuff as soon as the newspapers said there were drugs involved when the incident went down. The teachers all made little speeches about how much everybody would miss Bobby, but you could see it in their eyes that they believed all those lies in the paper and what they really wanted to say was "See what happens to you when you waste your potential and take drugs." And even though a bunch of kids tried to tell them that Bobby wasn't buying, nobody paid any attention to them. The police and the newspapers and the television reporters all commented and speculated that Bobby got caught buying a little recreational cocaine and *tsk tsk tsk* what a shame because he had so much potential. Even that Latina reporter from the TV station down in El Paso sat there in her sharp suit with her hair that doesn't move and pretended like she knew what she was talking about.

That's when I stopped reading newspapers and watching the TV news because those guys are supposed to be investigative reporters, but even an idiot like T.J. Richie could have made a better investigation than they did. All they would have had to do was go to my neighborhood and stand on the corner and watch. And they'd see that black pickup with the black tinted windows sitting right behind the bus stop. They'd see the bus pull up and all the kids start piling out the door and when the last couple of kids got off the bus, the door of that pickup would open and a real big guy in a black sweat suit with a black watch cap would get out and start walking behind those last kids. And the kids would walk a little bit faster and the blood in their ears would pound like that soundtrack from Jaws when the shark is circling the boat, getting ready to chomp their arms and legs off. And they'd see this one kid who was walking alone, like I made the mistake of doing a couple weeks after Bobby got popped. Then they'd see that big guy in the sweat suit grab that all-alone kid and put a gun up to his head and say, "Here's the package. Here's the address. Here's the money. Deliver it or you're dead." And the kid would deliver the package because he wasn't stupid enough to "Just Say No." And the next day, that kid would get the message that if he didn't show up on the corner and do another delivery, the cops would be knocking on his door to bust him for dealing drugs and they wouldn't believe him if he told them about the black pickup and the gun because he's a poor Mexican kid from a bad neighborhood so the cops figure he's theirs sooner or later and it might as well be sooner. And the kid would know that black truck would be waiting by the bus stop the next day, and he couldn't say no to drugs, so that kid and his cousins would make a gang and he would never have to walk alone again.

# Chapter 5

Okay, here's the difference between me and Harvey Castro who lives next door to me except it's like we live on different planets. He's friendly and everything, but we don't hang together because Harvey is a senior and I'm only a junior. Plus, Harvey is from Nicaragua which doesn't really matter except all the Anglo teachers think he's Mexican because he has black hair and speaks Spanish. Most Anglos are like that, but it isn't their fault because they don't get a very good education about us. In elementary school, they probably learn the Mexican hat dance and color in the geography maps for South American and Central America and memorize where the coffee beans come from. But by the time they get to high school, they don't know the difference between El Salvador and Ecuador. They read about two pages in the history book and then they forget all about south of the border except for the tequila and the drugs and the mariachi dancers and the coffee. Beecher told us she bought this special free trade coffee that was picked by people in Ecuador who didn't get ripped off by the big coffee companies. But I bet those people were still real poor because if they weren't, why would they spend all day picking coffee beans for rich Americans who spend so much money on one cup of coffee that they could have bought five breakfast burritos instead?

Anyway, Harvey is from Nicaragua so when he came here they put him in ESL class because he had a real big accent and nobody could understand him for about a year and after that they realized he was some kind of genius so they switched him to Advanced Placement where he has been kicking Anglo ass ever since.

Harvey is short and round and everybody calls him *Gordito* but he has a moustache and a girlfriend who has been engaged to him for two whole years. I'm tall and skinny and I have about three hairs on my chin and the longest I ever had a girlfriend was for one week. I met Silvia when I was working as a bagger at K-Mart over at White Sands Mall and she worked at Chik Fill-A. I probably wouldn't have even met her except we got off work at the same time and we both liked that bourbon chicken from the Chinese takeout. The first couple times I saw her, I didn't say anything because she was too pretty to talk to. But the third time I saw her, she brought her bourbon chicken over and sat down at the same little table where I was sitting and said, "Hi, I'm Silvia" and after that she was my girlfriend.

A couple days later, we were walking around the mall after work and Silvia said she was cold, so I bought her a leather jacket. The next day, she said she didn't want to miss my calls, so I bought her a cell phone. Then I didn't see her at work for a couple days so my cousin Graciela who is in the same class with Silvia drove me over to Tularosa where Silvia lives. When I knocked on the door, this big buff *guero* answered the door and told me to get lost and leave his girlfriend alone or he would mess me up good. I said what about all the stuff I bought her and he said, "That's your loss, sucker." He poked his finger in my chest, too, right in front of *mi prima*. I got so mad I drove like a maniac all the way home, and I drove into an irrigation ditch and hit a little tree and broke it. Graciela had to go to the hospital, but she was all right and she didn't sue me or anything because she's family and she felt sorry for me because it took me about six months to pay for that stupid tree. And now I have to walk or skateboard everyplace because Papi took my car away and gave me a bicycle which I wouldn't ride if you paid me because then everybody would see that I'm a loser.

Harvey Castro rides a bike. He rides it every single day even when it rains, but he never looks sweaty and his hair doesn't move. He has this kind of long hair that he combs straight back from his forehead and it never moves even in gym class. I think it looks wacked like those old TV game show guys, but all the girls think Harvey is cute. That's what they always say, "Ooh, Harvey is so cute." And if the guys make fun of Harvey for being cute, he just laughs and says, "Do you want my autograph now while you can still afford it?" No matter what anybody says to Harvey, he won't fight. He's too smart to fight. In fact, he should have been the valedictorian of his class when he graduates. I don't even know if I'm going to graduate or not. It depends. But Harvey already has a scholarship to go to University of New Mexico. He got invited to go to a bunch of other colleges, even some rich ones like Harvard, but he says he doesn't want to go too far away in case his parents need him for something.

Anyway, Harvey should be the valedictorian because he has a 5.0 GPA on account of all his extra credits for taking college classes and being president of the student council and all kinds of community service stuff that he didn't even have to do. The only time I ever did community service was when I got caught shoplifting. But last week, the principal called Harvey's parents and told them that they should be so proud of their son for being number two. Now he's the studitorian or some lame title like that. Even though everybody knows Harvey is *numero uno* and he has the highest GPA, it doesn't count because he was in ESL for a year and ESL credits don't count the same as regular classes. So they took away being the valedictorian. Harvey's mother called up my mother and told her all about it and I thought *Hijole! Watch out!* because now Harvey is going to let them have it but the next day he just walked around like normal. He didn't even act like he was pissed.

Henry Dominguez asked Harvey was he going to sue the school and Harvey just laughed and said, "It's just high school. It doesn't really matter."

That's the real difference between Harvey and me. Things don't matter to him like they do to me. I would of burned down the school or at least tore a toilet off the wall in the bathroom. But that's why I'm in the alt school and Harvey Castro isn't, even though I used to get straight A's before I started being a juvenile delinquent. Harvey's parents are poor just like mine, and he's the oldest kid in a big family just like me, and he's Catholic and his father kicks his ass just like Papi does mine, so how come Harvey's so cool and I'm so hot? How come he just walks away from fights and does his homework and gets a college scholarship and I attract fights like mosquitoes on a summer night? Is it in my genes? Or did my parents do something wrong? Or am I just who I am by accident?

I used to think I was messed up because of being a sex offender in the second grade. I wasn't really a sex offender but that's what the school labeled me after I kicked my teacher in the crotch. I didn't mean to kick her in the crotch, neither. I was just trying to get her to let go of my ear. She was this real mean little teacher who used to twist the boys' ears all the time, anytime we did even the littlest thing wrong, and sometimes when we didn't even do anything. She would just grab your ear and twist it until it felt like she was ripping it right off your head and we would all cry, even T.J. Ritchie, because it hurt real bad. And this one day, I had a ear infection and I even had a note from my mother saying I shouldn't have to take gym class and that teacher knew I had a ear infection but she twisted my ear anyway. I yelled at her to stop but she wouldn't. And I tried to hit her but my arms were too short. She just held her arm out straight and practically picked me up off the floor by my ear. So I kicked her. I wasn't aiming at any special place. I just kicked and my foot went right between her legs.

It was a total accident. I didn't even know where I kicked her. I was just glad she finally let go of my ear. But the next thing you know, they had the security guards and the police and the psychologist and the nurse and everybody all interrogating me and asking me questions. I can't even remember what they asked me because my ear hurt so much that mostly I just nodded my head because I didn't want to say anything because then I would start crying like a little baby in front of all those people.

They put me out of school for a week and when I came back, all the kids acted like I was Rambo or something. T.J. Ritchie said I was a real bad ass and I thought that was so cool, so I pretended like I meant to kick that teacher. And I said I would kick her again if she came near me so they put me in another teacher's room and I could tell right away that she was afraid of me and I thought how cool is that, a teacher being afraid of you when you're only seven years old. So every time she looked at me, I messed up my face and tried to look like a real mean bad-ass.

After that, they started sending me to talk to this lady in a suit every Friday when we were supposed to have recess and she asked me to draw pictures and play with toys and make up stories about all kinds of weird things like what would I do if I had a little baby and I was the father and would I punch that baby if it cried. I liked that lady because she had a nice soft voice and she never yelled or twisted my ears. At the end of second grade, I never saw that lady again but when I went to third grade, they put me in special ed. Not the special ed for dumb kids but the special ed for kids who don't know how to act. I told them I already knew how to act but nobody listened to me, so I showed them I could act like those idiots. I drew pictures of *chichis* on my desk and threw gummy bears up so they stuck on the lights and sneezed *mocos* all over the hair of the girl who sat in front of me—then they started making me take those pills. I took them for a couple of months but they made me feel spastic, so I started throwing them away until T.J. Ritchie told me I could sell them.

It really wasn't such a big deal. I could have kept on telling those people what happened until somebody believed me. Or I could have just said I was sorry for kicking that teacher and started getting A's again, but I was too stubborn and so mad. Even way back then when I was little, I was mad about how they treat boys different. When girls do mean things, people always think they were abused or something. When a boy does something mean, even by accident, people usually think he's a future felon, especially if the boy is Mexican.

Still, I could have brushed it all off just like Harvey Castro brushed off getting his valedictorian award stolen by the school. But I can't brush off anything. Not even little stuff. Everything just sticks to me. And all those little things just weigh me down so much that I feel like my bones are made of stone and if I walked into the Rio Grande, I would sink to the bottom so fast that I wouldn't even make a ripple and nobody would even notice I was gone.

# Chapter 6

T.J. Ritchie is a no-brain stoner, but you got to give him props for having big *cojones*. T.J. just says what he thinks no matter what. Part of the reason is because he's so big, I think, but the other part is because he really believes he has everything figured out. Like yesterday, when we were discussing current events in McElroy's class, and this one black kid said what about that black guy who didn't do nothing and didn't even have a gun and he got killed by the cops right before he was supposed to get married and why does that shit keep happening, T.J. said, "Because *you* people let it happen, dipshit."

Everybody started hollering different stuff at T.J. and the black kid looked around real fast, like he was looking for his homies to back him up except if you're black in Rosablanca, you're on your own. We only got like six black kids in the whole school. McElroy banged his ruler on his desk which is the signal for everybody to stop talking, but T.J. kept right on going.

"I'm serious," T.J. said. "The cops don't do nothing about it and the government sure ain't gonna do nothing about it, so the regular good black people need to do something about it. Whenever a cop kills a innocent black guy who wasn't even strapped, then some other regular black people need to kill that cop. If the cop kills two black guys, they need to kill that cop and his partner so they'll know how it feels to get killed just for being who you are. If they can't get to the cop, they should kill his wife or one of his kids. And don't just shoot them once, neither. They got to shoot them forty or fifty times, because that's what the cops do to those guys. You know the guy is dead after the first or second shot, but they keep on shooting and shooting so the guy can't get better and sue them. *Bang bang bang bang bang bang bang bang bang bang.* Dead dead dead dead dead dead dead dead dead dead dead—"

"Shut up!" Teeny White covered her ears. "You're crazy. You're making me sick." And a bunch of other kids started yelling at T.J. to shut up because he was advocating hate crimes. McElroy tried to act like he was in charge of everything. He huffed up to his desk and wrote T.J. a referral to the office, but T.J. just crumpled up the referral and threw it on the floor. He stood up and kicked the back of his chair so hard that one of the bolts came loose and the chair sort of flopped sideways like T.J. had killed it, too.

"I ain't advocating nothing," T.J. said. "I'm just saying if you want people to understand how something feels, sometimes you have to do the same thing to them. Like if we could lock all the teachers in one big room and treat them like shit, maybe some of them would stop acting like such fucking jerks to us." He glared at McElroy who ran over to the red phone and called Security. T.J. just laughed and shook his head and pointed at McElroy. "See what I'm talking about? Can't even have an honest discussion about anything. If you don't say what they want, or if you treat them like they treat you, they beat you down or lock you up."

T.J. walked over to the doorway and slammed himself up against the wall and held his arms out in front with his wrists together like he was waiting to get handcuffed. When Security showed up, it was just the little blonde lady guard. She looks like a kid, but up close you can tell she's old enough to be your mother. They always send her to get T.J. because they probably think he wouldn't beat up a female, especially a old one. He would if he wanted to, though. I know he would, except then he would go to real jail instead of just juvi where he has a lot of friends so he doesn't care. He won't even get sent to juvi for killing a chair and being disruptive, though. He'll just get a three-day vacation which is supposed to give him time to think about his behavior and realize he needs to learn some anger management skills, but he'll just sit at home and drink his dad's beer and smoke some dope and play video games and watch some porn if he can find his dad's new hiding place.

When the Security lady walked in, T.J. slammed himself up against the wall again and held out his wrists, but the lady just laughed and pointed to the door. T.J. took a couple steps and then turned back around and said, "You guys should think about what I said. If I was a black guy and I said all that shit, you know they would lock me up like they did Huey Newton or kill me like they did Malcolm X. But I'm white and I don't even like black people that much."

T.J. shot a look at the black kid and shoved his hands into his pockets. "Sorry, but that's just how I am. I say what a lot of people are probably thinking and everybody can pretend they didn't think it and call me crazy and stupid. And maybe my idea is crazy, but it isn't stupid. I'm not stupid."

"That's enough," McElroy told us after T.J. finally followed the security lady outside, but nobody was talking. We were all trying not to look at the black kid. And I could tell that some of the other kids were thinking about T.J.'s idea like I was. I mean, I don't think killing people is such a great idea, especially cops, because then your life is really over. But in a way T.J. was right. Teachers ask us to have a discussion but then if they don't like what we say, they tell us to shut up. And he's right about making people think, too. Sometimes you got to knock people down and shove the other guy's shoes onto their feet before they will walk a mile in them.

T.J. looked different walking beside that little security guard. He didn't look small, because he's too big to look small, but even from the back, you could tell he knew everybody was watching him get walked by Security. Like he was walking beside his grandmother or like he was walking beside a real cop.

You walk different when you walk beside a cop because it's like you can see yourself and you think, *Do I look like a rat who just turned on his homies to save his ass?* or *Do I look like a pervert who just passed by the elementary school with his pants unzipped and his dog hanging out?* I hope I don't look like somebody stupid enough to sell meth because that shit is death, man. I'm pretty sure I don't look like a cop, even a undercover cop, because cops have a look in their eyes like if you mess up, I will rip your liver out and eat it for lunch. I don't think that's what my eyes say, even when I try to look all kick-ass. The worst my eyes probably say is "maybe I'm not that good of a fighter but I go down hard."

I walked with a cop once, right here at Bright Horizons. I wasn't getting arrested or anything. I was being an escort. Beecher wrote to the police and asked them did they want to come over and give a pep talk to her class so we might decide to stop being juvenile delinquents. We didn't think the cops would come—hey, that reminds me of this baseball cap *mi primo* Enrique used to wear all the time that says, "Call 911. Make a cop come." He had to stop wearing it because the cops didn't think it was too funny. Anyways, we didn't think the cops would waste their time talking to us, especially since most of us already did too much talking to the cops out on the street, but Beecher got a letter from this one cop, Sergeant Chris Cabrera, who said he would be honored to be our guest speaker.

Beecher picked me to escort Sgt. Cabrera from the office to our room because I made the mistake of telling T.J. Ritchie to shut up after he said, "Oh, goody. I'm going to take notes when he's talking so I can learn how to be a better person." I told T.J. to get a little respect because Cabrera could have just flipped us off and Beecher said, "Eddie is absolutely right." And then she asked me to stay after class so she could explain my escort duties.

"Hey, you're a male escort," Henry Dominguez said.

"Men don't call male escorts, you idiot," T.J. said and Teeny White said, "Uh-huh. Some of them do," but Beecher cut that discussion off at the neck because she could see where it was headed. And when Sgt. Cabrera showed up and the office called me to come and get him, he turned out to be a she. It used to be all the cops were men but now they got girl cops in all kind of sizes and even the little ones can kick your butt pretty good with their bare hands.

Sgt. Cabrera wasn't little. She was taller than me, probably 5' 10", and she looked like she might do a little weight training on the side because she had her sleeves rolled up and her biceps were pretty cut and you could see the veins bulging on her wrists just like the bodybuilders. She told me she was from Puerto Rico but everybody thinks she's Mexican because she lives in New Mexico, even the Mexicans. I told her they should know better because she doesn't sound Mexican to me. She sounds like New York and she said, "Bingo!" and aimed her hand at me like a gun and shot me except she was smiling so I shot her back.

"What are you going to do after you graduate?" she asked me right before we got to Beecher's room. I told her I wasn't sure I would graduate because of various things and she said, "You mean you haven't decided to make it happen?" and she nodded like she knew everything about me. I was glad we got to the room right after that because, even though she was friendly and everything, it made me feel nervous when she looked me in the eye. She didn't have the rip-your-liver-out look. She had a nice look, kind of like Beecher, except Sgt. Cabrera's look had some kind of extra power, like x-ray vision or something, and you could tell she could cut right through whatever shit you tried to throw at her. All during her talk, I felt like she was staring at me, even though she probably wasn't. I stayed in my seat when everybody was clapping after she finished inspiring us, hoping that Beecher would just let Sgt. Cabrera walk back to the office herself since she knew where it was, but both of them stood there and smiled at me, so I had to be her escort again.

I thought Sgt. Cabrera would give me a lecture or maybe ask me a bunch of questions on the way to the office, but she didn't. She just asked me did I like to read and I said, "Yes, only please don't tell anybody because I got a reputation to maintain," and she said I should read *The Four Agreements* by this guy named Don Miguel Ruiz.

"It's a real short book," she said, "and it sounds too simple, but if you really think about what it says, you realize it's very deep and it can change your life."

I nodded, but I didn't say what I was thinking which was that my life could use some change but not the kind you get from reading a little book. My life would need an encyclopedia.

"It might even make you decide to graduate." Sgt. Cabrera winked at me like we had some big secret going and I was glad there was nobody else around.

"It's not up to me," I said. "I don't have enough credits and I'm flunking biology."

"You're only a junior," Sgt. Cabrera said. "You have a whole summer and another year ahead of you. Why not think positive? Your thoughts create your intentions and your intentions create your reality." She winked at me again. "That's from the book."

"Yeah, thanks," I said and then I walked faster so I could get that crazy cop to the office and get rid of her. She must have gone to high school or they wouldn't let her join the police, but she must have forgot what it's like. If you want to graduate high school, you have to be a liar. You have to pretend you care about stuff you don't care about, like what does a frog's guts look like and how to multiply fractions, and you have to keep your mouth shut when you feel like talking, but then you have to talk when you don't feel like it, except you have to say what you're supposed to say and not what you really think. You have to wear clothes you don't like and act respectful to people who need a good punch in the face.

Papi is always telling me to just act like I respect everybody and life will be easier. Like he always tells me to just shut up and do what the teachers tell me, and I won't have any more troubles. And I know he tells me to keep my big fat *boca* shut because he can't do it, neither, which is why he doesn't have a job right now. He always gets hired on construction crews when they first start up because he's big and fast. He can swing a hammer with both hands so good that he only needs one hit per nail and if they put him on one end of a two-by-twelve and a guy with a nail gun on the other end, they end up meeting in the middle. But if the boss talks down to him or says one thing about wetbacks or beaners or sometimes if they even just ask if anybody wants Taco Bell for lunch, Papi just flips the guy off and picks up his lunch pail and heads for his truck. And the next time that foreman needs a crew, Papi doesn't even try to get on because he would have to say he was sorry when he wasn't.

If it wasn't for my mother, I wouldn't even stay in school for one second, but I promised her I would graduate and set a good example for Letty and my little brothers and cousins. Being a good example is hard work, but at least it makes me feel like I'm doing something and not just taking up space. I'd like to take up a real big space some day, so big that people would have to stand back when I walk into the room, but I would act like I didn't even notice they were looking at me. That way, people wouldn't feel embarrassed and they could take a good long look at me and maybe they would see something in me that is so good I can't even see it myself.

# Chapter 7

Yo, I finally got a girlfriend. A real one, too, not the kind you have to pay just so you can touch her. And I didn't even have to use any of the pickup lines Primo made me practice for two weeks after Silvia turned out not to be my girlfriend.

"You got to act like you notice a woman," Enrique said, "and you got to let her know you think she's fine, but not so fine that she could have you just like that." He snapped his fingers and stuck his chin up in the air. He thinks that makes him look like a *chingon* movie star, but it really makes him look just like that little bobble-head Chihuahua he glued to the dashboard of his Camaro.

Anyway, I didn't have to say anything cool or walk like a panther or flash my new cell phone or anything. All I did was sign up for ballroom dance. I could have signed up last semester when Beecher tried to get a bunch of us guys to sign up, but back then I thought ballroom dancing was too gay for a guy like me.

"You can get the fine arts credits you need to graduate and you will meet lots of girls," Beecher told us. "And let me tell you, girls love to dance. They don't care if you don't dance very well. They will like you just for trying." But we still wouldn't do it. At first, T.J. Ritchie said he was going to, so some other guys said they would, too, but then T.J. snorted and spit a big wet one into the trash can and said, "You pussies have a good time," so nobody signed up.

This semester, I decided to give it a try after I watched "So You Think You Can Dance" because, even though I don't know if I can dance, all the girls on that show looked so fine.

I didn't think the girls at Bright Horizons would be as fine as the girls on television, but at least they would be real live girls and I would get to look at them up close and hold their hands while we were dancing.

There was only three guys in the whole class and twenty-three girls. At first, I was thinking I would just ask for a bathroom pass and never come back, but the teacher was standing way on the other side of the gym and I didn't want to walk across that whole floor and ask to go to the bathroom with all those girls watching me because you know how girls are. They were standing real close to each other and giggling and grabbing each other and pretending they were interested in what each other was saying when all the time what they were really doing was checking out the dudes. All except this one girl who was sort of standing off to the side by herself. Not like she was stuck-up or shy. Just like she was the kind of girl who could stand alone and not care about it.

I was so busy looking at the girls that I didn't even realize I was walking until I got halfway across the floor to where the teacher and the girls were standing. Then I got close enough to see that all-alone girl's eyes, and she was looking right at me and not even pretending she wasn't. I stopped walking and just stood there looking at her and, I'm not kidding, the lights in the gym brightened up like the sun was shining down from the basketball hoop. And the sunlight sparkled on that girl and made her shine like an angel. Just like in the movies. I always thought they made up that romantic shit, but I guess you just think that if you never got struck down by love.

Finally, I noticed that everybody was looking at me, even the teacher, who was this little *gordita* lady with her red hair in a bun and a real tight stretchy black shirt and pants and black high heels with little pink socks just like the ones Letty wears with lace around the tops.

"Welcome to ballroom dance," the lady said. "I'm Mrs. Martinez." She looked down at the clipboard she was holding and then looked at me. "You must be Eduardo Corazon."

"Eddie," I said. I could hardly make myself stop looking at the girl and look at the teacher who turned out to be Mexican. From far away, you couldn't tell because of her red hair but, up close, you could see that she was born with black hair. But she didn't look like one of those *Mejicanas* who change their hair to make themselves look Anglo. She just wanted to look special. I could just see her standing in the back of the Dollar Store, choosing those pink socks and humming a little song and smiling, doing a little *cha-cha* on the way to the cash register.

At first, Mrs. Martinez made the boys stand in a line across from the girls so she could show us how to make a frame with our arms so we could guide the ladies firmly and smoothly through the box step. She made us dance with her, one at a time, so she could make sure we didn't have noodle arms. Then, everybody had to count out loud and do the steps. "One and two, three. One and two, three." The girls all got it right away and so did I. It was real easy, just like doing the *cumbia* in a square, but the other two boys were Anglo and they acted like it was harder than algebra. So Mrs. Martinez called me to the front to demonstrate the steps. I thought she was going to dance with me, but she picked up her clipboard and said, "Now I need a young lady to be your partner." Before Mrs. Martinez could even look at her clipboard, that all-alone girl just walked out and stood in front of me, face to face, so close, I could smell her hair which smelled exactly like an angel.

"Why, thank you, Lupe," Mrs. Martinez said and she smiled like the *viejas* at church when they catch you having lustful thoughts when you're supposed to be listening to the priest. When Mrs. Martinez told Lupe to put her left hand on my right shoulder and told me to put my left hand on Lupe's waist, my inside self started jumping up and down and screaming, "Yes! Yes! Yes!" but outside, I just smiled and stood up as tall as I could to make a good frame for Lupe.

After we did the box step about ten times, Mrs. Martinez clapped her hands and everybody had to find a partner and practice. The girls started giggling again and a couple of them grabbed those Anglo boys real quick while Lupe and I just stood there, holding our frame and our breath, waiting to see if Mrs. Martinez would make us change partners. She didn't make us change right then, but after we practiced a little bit more, she clapped her hands and said, "Change partners!" and we had to because she was standing right beside us.

Before that class was over, I danced with every single girl. Twenty-three. I touched more girls in that forty-five minutes than I touched in my whole life up until that day. It was one of the best days I ever had, and the best part was that as soon as class was over, Lupe asked me did I know where Mr. McElroy's room was. She just transferred to Bright Horizons which is why I had never seen her around before. I had been wondering because I would have noticed Lupe, even if there had been a million girls at school.

I told Lupe I was going to McElroy's class so I could walk her over there and for a minute, I even thought about holding out my elbow like when you have to help the *viejas* get down the aisle to their favorite pew. I walked down the hall so proud beside Lupe. She tossed her hair over her shoulder and a little piece touched my cheek and I wished I could put my whole face in her hair and breathe her right inside of me where I would take care of her forever.

When we got to McElroy's room, he didn't even yell at me for being late because I brought Lupe, but he made me sit in the empty chair in the front row where you have to sit if you get busted for sleeping or passing notes. I didn't even care, because he put Lupe in the desk right behind me. Every couple of minutes, I turned just a little bit so McElroy wouldn't notice, until I was sitting sideways and I could see Lupe out of the corner of my eye. And that was the first time I wished English class was longer. I could have sat there forever.

At lunch, I asked Lupe why she was at the alt school because she looked real smart and she didn't dress like a gangbanger or anything, and she said she got kicked out of Rosablanca High because there was this one girl named Cheyenne who kept starting fights with her. I knew exactly which Cheyenne she was talking about. Cheyenne used to be in my class when I was in Special Ed because she flunked first grade for not being able to read and then the next year, she kept banging her head against the wall whenever the teacher asked her to read.

"I don't even know her," Lupe said. "She would just come up and hit me. And she would send her friends over to hit me, too, and then they would tell the teachers that I started it by calling them 'retards,' so nobody believed me. Even when I had witnesses. Finally, I told my mother to just pretend she believed them so they would transfer me over here."

I told Lupe that me and my cousins would go and beat those girls down, but she freaked so bad she almost started crying. "No!" she said. "Then they would say I instigated that, too, and I would get in more trouble. I just want to go to school and do my work and graduate so I can go to college."

I could see why a girl would want to beat Lupe down, especially a big ugly stupid girl. Lupe looks kind of like Selma Hayek and her hair shines even more than Beecher's and she has those perfect round *chichis* that are the exact fit for my hand and a nice fat little butt that looks exactly like an upside down heart. She looks just as good from the back as she does from the front. Plus, she's the smartest girl in class, maybe even smarter than Harvey Castro. She's going to go to college and be an obstatician so she can help women have babies that don't die from not having enough nutrition like her *Tia* Gloria's did.

"Where are you going to college?" Lupe asked me and I told her I wasn't sure. I didn't tell her I won't even graduate unless I start going to after-school tutoring and even then I'll probably have to go to summer school, too. I told her I was still considering my options and she said, "Good. The more education you have, the more options you have." She sounded just like Beecher which only proves that Lupe is smart enough to be a teacher even if she's only sixteen. In fact, she's smart enough to figure out how to get out of Bright Horizons and back to the regular high school if she wanted to but when I told her that, she said she'd rather stay here where she can work in the computer lab and go as fast as she wants to and just take the final exam after she's done learning something, instead of always having to wait for all the immature obnoxious children who still think school is a big joke.

"You mean like me?" I said and Lupe laughed. "No, not you. You aren't obnoxious. You're just confused. But you're smart."

"How do you know I'm smart?" I said and Lupe said, "You were smart enough to pick me out of all those girls in ballroom dance class, weren't you?" And she smiled at me because we both know that Lupe is the one who did the picking and I'm the one who got picked.

"Men just think they run things," Lupe told me when we were eating lunch. I was real hungry and for a minute I forgot about making a good impression. I had just shoved half a burrito into my mouth and it was too full of beans and cheese to argue with her.

"Women just let men think they're in charge because it makes you happy," Lupe said. "And you're so cute when you're happy."

Right then, Primo sneaked up and smacked me on the back which made me spit little bits of cheesy beans all over the cafeteria table. I started coughing and Enrique kept pounding me on the back and saying, "You want me to do the Hemlicker on you?"

Every time Enrique said "Hemlicker," Lupe said, "It's Heimlich," and Enrique said, "Whatever." After the third time, he gave Lupe such a mean look that I pointed to my watch and pointed towards the door so she would just leave and not be late for class. She asked me was I all right and I tried to say, "I'm fine," but that made me cough again.

"See what you did?" Lupe said to Enrique and he just balled up his fists and walked away. The next time I saw him, he told me I was whipped and I shouldn't be so nice to Lupe because women don't respect men who are too nice to them. I told Enrique that me and Lupe respect each other and he was just jealous because Lupe was so much smarter than him. He said, "Oh, yeah? If she was smart, she would of played you a little bit instead of just jumping into your arms. Besides, if she's so great, she would of already had a boyfriend."

"Haven't you ever heard of love at first sight?" I asked him and he said, "Haven't you ever heard that guys like the hunt better than the kill? Everybody knows that us guys want what they can't have. If deers just walked up and let people shoot them, nobody would go hunting any more."

"Yeah, well, I hate hunting," I said. "And I like Lupe and she likes me. And she didn't have a boyfriend because she's serious about school. And besides, she wouldn't pretend not to like somebody that she did like. That would be stupid."

"Whatever," Enrique said. "But I still say you're whipped."

I don't think I'm whipped, but even if I am, I don't care because I'm happy. I don't want what I can't have, except if I couldn't have Lupe, I would still want her. I wouldn't just forget about her like I forgot about Silvia and all those other girls I used to want before I realized it's stupid to want somebody who doesn't want you back. I don't care if all the other guys want what they can't have. I want what I have and I have what I want. I got Lupe.

# Chapter 8

I can't believe it. I actually wrote some poems. Beecher tried to get me to write some last year after she caught me reading this one library book that had a bunch of poems by Gary Soto, but I wouldn't do it just like I wouldn't sign up for ballroom dance back then. But last week when Lupe said she thought poets were deep, I decided I better give it a try—especially since T.J. Ritchie wrote a poem that Mr. McElroy typed up and sent to a magazine because he said it was so good. I can't have T.J. going around looking deeper than me, especially in front of Lupe.

When I told Lupe I was thinking about writing a poem, she clapped her hands and kissed me on the mouth, right in the hallway. Then I had to do it, except I couldn't think of a subject. So I looked it up in our literature book where there is a chapter on poetry. In the writing assignment part, it said anything could inspire a poem, it doesn't have to be nature or love or death or big important things. You can just look around at the world and paint word pictures of what you see like a red wheelbarrow. So, I looked around McElroy's room at the punks and stoners and assorted losers and the bulletin boards and all the lame posters that are supposed to inspire you because they have a picture of an airplane crashing through a bunch of clouds and a quotation underneath the airplane that is supposed to make you want to be a successful person instead of a high school drop-out. Then I wrote two poems, just like that. Here they are:

## ALTERNATIVE EDUCATION

*I read a quotation that said*
*"when the student is ready, the teacher appears"*
*and I was thinking*
*sometimes I need to learn something*
*except I'm not really ready*
*but the teacher appears anyway*
*so I ditch that class*
*and go smoke behind the gym.*
*Most of the teachers don't care if I'm gone*
*but one teacher will follow me out to the gym*
*and she won't bust me for smoking*
*or tell me how cigarettes can kill me.*
*Instead, she'll watch me smoke a little while.*
*Then she'll hand me a flute and say*
*"Why don't you play me a song?"*

Okay. That was number one. I still haven't decided whether I like it or not because it has such a weird ending. But I didn't even make up that ending. It just came out of my pencil. Anyway, here's number two. I don't have a good title for it, so right now I'm just calling it "Pierce Everything."

## PIERCE EVERYTHING

*Punk up your hair or shave your head*
*Pierce your eyebrows and your nipples*
*and your lips and your soul*
*So the hate and the hurt can ooze out of you*
*through a million tiny holes*

I got some tears in my eyes after I wrote that one, but lucky for me nobody saw because the bell rang for lunch while I was writing and everybody except Lupe ran out of the room, including McElroy who always goes jogging during lunch in some baggy brown shorts. Lupe stayed at her desk, but she wasn't looking at me. She was copying down the assignment from the white board and she had her head bent down close to her notebook. It almost looked like she was praying and her hair fell down and hid her face like a shiny black satin curtain. And Lupe became my next poem.

### LUPE FULL OF GRACE

*I wish I could be Lupe's rosary*
*so she could hold me in her hands*
*and tangle me up in her fingers*
*and press me to her lips*
*and pray me into being a good man*
*one bead at a time*

After I wrote that, I felt like I had turned into a poem myself. I felt as light as a piece of paper, like I could float right up to the ceiling. I copied that poem over real neat and tore the page out of my notebook and folded it over and over, like the little kids do, until it was a tiny little square. I wrote Lupe's initials on it and put it in my pocket and carried it around with me until after school when I pretended to tickle Lupe and I stuck it inside her bra and held her hands so she couldn't get it out. When I finally let go, she hit me in the head with her purse and called me a *pachuco*, but I didn't even care. I just smiled, thinking of my poem, sitting so close to Lupe's heart.

# Chapter 9

After Lupe read my poems, she cried. Then she told me I should be a writer because "if you can write something that makes people cry, then you have the gift." I told Lupe maybe I had a little tiny gift. Maybe only she would cry from reading my poems and not other people, so she said, "Let's show them to Mr. McElroy and see what he thinks" and I said, "Not."

"You shouldn't be afraid," Lupe said. "He's not a very good teacher, but he's a nice man. And he wouldn't laugh at you, if that's what you're thinking."

"I'm not afraid he would laugh at me," I said, except that is exactly what I was thinking. "I just don't want to show them to nobody but you."

We were sitting on the bench outside the main office eating lunch where most kids don't like to hang out because it's too close to the principal. There are other places where it would be more private, but I don't trust myself to be in private places with Lupe at school. When we're in the same class, sometimes I have to get myself kicked out because sometimes I can't sit down when Lupe's in the same room with me— if you know what I mean. I have to get out of the room just so I can breathe.

"Your poems are better than T.J. Ritchie's poem that got sent to the magazine," Lupe said. "He showed it to me. Yours are way better."

I didn't like T.J. showing his poem to my girlfriend, but at least she liked mine better than his. Unless she was just trying to give me self-esteem which she thinks is so important if you want to succeed in life. Beecher was always talking about self-esteem, too, and how you can program your brain to succeed because your brain doesn't know when you're lying. Like if you keep telling yourself, "I am a intelligent successful person," your brain will believe you even though your brain is sitting right there where it could see that you're a stupid loser if it took a good look.

I believed Lupe liked my poem better, though, because she never lies to me even though *mi primo* Enrique says you can never trust a woman. Plus, I read T.J.'s poem and it wasn't that good, even though it was better than some of the poems in our literature book.

Everybody acted all surprised when they found out T.J. wrote a real poem because T.J. makes a big deal out of not living up to his potential and being disruptive and anti-social. But he's a secret reader, just like me, except he's even more secret than I am. If somebody asks me do I like to read, I say, "Yeah," and then I give them a look that tells them they better not ask me what I like to read because this ain't Oprah's book club. But T.J. pretends he doesn't even know how to read. If a teacher tries to make him read out loud in class, T.J. will either read like he's in kindergarten, pushing his big dirty finger across the page and reading one word at a time or else he'll say, "Reading sucks," and he'll say "suck" real dirty so it sounds like the other "uck" word, so the teacher will send him to the office for using inappropriate language.

T.J. reads real books when nobody is looking, though. I caught him myself. Once, I saw him reading a book behind the bleachers when we were both cutting first period math. When I walked past, T.J. dropped the book on the ground and put his foot on it like he didn't know it was there and he asked me did I have a cigarette. I said sorry I just smoked my last one even though I don't smoke because I'm not stupid enough to think lung cancer is cool just because they put a camel or a cowboy on the commercial. Right then, one of the security guards slammed open the gym door and let it slam shut real loud to let us know that if we didn't get back to class, we'd get busted. So T.J. left that book laying right in the dirt. I got a bathroom pass the next period and took a little detour behind the bleachers on my way and that book was still there. It wasn't porn or a comic book, like I expected. It was a real book—*The Curious Incident of the Dog in the Night Time*. I read the first page just to see what kind of a book would have a title like that and it turned out to be about this kid who everybody thought was stupid except he was really smart in some ways. Like he couldn't have a conversation with anybody but he could multiply real big numbers in his head like that guy in "Rain Man." He reminded me of a lot of the kids in Special Ed who aren't as stupid as the teachers think they are.

The next thing I knew I read the whole book so I must have sat out there for a couple of hours. I got detention for cutting but I didn't care because I wanted some quiet time to think about that book. I had never read anything like it before. That weekend, I went to the bookstore and asked the lady did she have any more books by the guy who wrote that one. She said no but she asked me if I wanted to try another book with an unusual title and she gave me *The Lone Ranger and Tonto Fist Fight in Heaven* by the same Indian guy who wrote the story that Beecher read us. After I read those two books, I realized there are two kinds of books in the world – the boring kind they make you read in school and the interesting kind that they won't let you read in school because then they would have to talk about real stuff like sex and divorce and is there a God and if there isn't, then what happens when you die, and how come the history books have so many lies in them. They make us read the boring books so the teachers just have to talk about safe stuff like amoebas and tse-tse flies and the hypotenuse of a triangle and all those things which nobody cares about in real life.

The warning bell rang to let everybody know it was time to stop eating lunch and enjoying themselves and get back to earning an education, so Lupe gathered up all her stuff and shoved it in her backpack. I was so busy watching her move because she is so graceful like a flamenco dancer with hands that can become a flying dove or a flower opening up its petals, so I didn't realize Lupe also put my notebook with the poems into her backpack until she said, "I have your poems and I'm going to show them to Mr. McElroy unless you get down on your knees and beg me to give them back to you."

I would do anything for Lupe. I would kill for her. But there is no way I get on my knees for anything—except to ask Lupe to marry me which I'm going to do someday but not until I have a good job so I can take care of her. I told Lupe go ahead because I didn't care if she showed my poems to McElroy but don't tell him I wrote them. I don't want him reading them out loud in front of everybody and saying I wrote them because I have a reputation to maintain. Lupe laughed and gave me back my notebook.

"I wasn't really going to show them to anybody," she said. "They're too personal. I just wanted to see how brave you really are." She squeezed my bicep and pretended to be surprised at how buff I am in spite of being so skinny. "Ooh. He's smart and sensitive and strong *and* fearless," she said. She ran her fingers up my arm and touched my lips with her finger. Then she put the finger on her own lips and kissed it which made me dizzy. And the next thing I knew, I was sitting in McElroy's class where we had to write a five-paragraph essay.

"Tell me what you're going to tell me," he said. "Then, tell me. Then, tell me what you told me. It's simple."

It's simple, all right. And boring. And stupid. And pointless. But you have to write the essay to pass the exam so you can graduate and the teacher won't get fired. I was going to write about music and how it can make you smart which is something that Beecher taught us. She said if you listen to certain music, you get smarter. And some music makes plants grow better. I looked it up on the Internet to see if she was just playing us, but she was telling the truth. There was all kinds of articles and scientific reports about how classical music makes you smart but heavy metal and rap can screw up your head. I stopped listening to rap after that. I never liked it much anyway, but I liked driving around with my homies with the windows down, playing rap music loud enough to break your head, wearing shades and staring down all the old people who would roll up their car windows real fast like they were scared we were going to carjack them right in front of Taco Time. I believe those articles because if you listen to metal or rap really loud, like in a car that has sixteen batteries in the trunk to juice the speakers, after a while you get a feeling like you just won a fight or kissed a girl or something, except you didn't do anything. You get this rush, like chemicals in your blood and you feel like you had some real feelings except you didn't have to feel them.

That's what I was going to write about, but McElroy said we had to write about his topic which was politics. I used to didn't care about politics because it doesn't make any difference to me if the President wears a red neck tie or a blue one. Then I heard the President giving a speech on television and he said he doesn't listen to his father because his father doesn't tell him what to do. So, I figured he might be all right because I don't listen to Papi, neither. But then the President said he talks to God and God tells him what to do. I kept expecting somebody to jump up and scream, "It's

Saturday Night Live!" but it was for real. So I wondered how come they don't make him stop being President. Because if the president of some other country went on TV and said he gets messages from Allah or some kind of foreign god who doesn't speak English, Americans would freak out and think he was a lunatic and assassinate him or put economic sanctions on him. So, I looked the President up on the Internet and that's when I found this web site called Common Dreams and that's where I read that one of the new political plans is to get rid of all the Mexicans.

Everybody knows the Anglos are nervous about Mexicans having so many kids and taking over the country. But they didn't really think it could happen until one day they counted up the people and California was half Hispanic. New Mexico is probably more than half Hispanic, too, but New Mexicans aren't stupid enough to stand still and let people count us. And we know how to get along in New Mexico. If you want to rub elbows with mostly Anglos and speak English, move down to Cruces. If you want to speak Spanish, move over to Deming or up to Espanola. If you like to mix it up a little, then you got a bunch of little towns in the middle to pick from like Tularosa, Socorro, and Truth or Consequences.

I don't blame the Anglos for being worried about so many Mexicans because they know payback is a bitch and we got a lot of payback coming to us. And if we ever joined up with our Indian and black brothers, the Anglos would have to circle those wagon trains for real. But we wouldn't kill the Anglos which is what they think. We wouldn't torture them, neither, or make them slaves or make them speak a different language because we know how much that kind of stuff sucks. We wouldn't rape all the white women, either. We wouldn't have to. A lot of white women like dark men. They know we like sports, just like the *gueros*, but the brown brothers won't pass up a hot woman to watch a game on TV. We know how to hit the "Record" button on our VCRs.

So, we won't kill the *gueros*. We'll just put them to work. We'll make them be the cooks and the janitors and the car washers and the lawn mowers and the sewer diggers. We'll pay them two dollars an hour and fire them if they take a day off to take their kid to the hospital. We'll talk to them in Spanish and if they don't understand us, we'll say it louder and slower, and shake our heads because how stupid can you be not to be able to speak such a simple language. In Spanish, you say the letters in all the words just like they look. A is always *ah*, and E is always *aye*, and I is always *eee*. We don't have six different ways to say the same letters like *dough* and *thought* and *through* and *tough* which all have "o-u" but different pronunciations, so that when you're trying to learn English you sound stupid no matter how smart you are.

We'll make the Anglos live in falling-down trailers and work in the fields picking chiles fourteen hours a day, even when it's a hundred and ten degrees. We'll feel real sorry for them and maybe even appreciate them. We'll say, "I don't know how you can stand the heat. You people are so strong," and we'll pretend we believe they have a choice. We'll pretend we like them, too. We'll make statues of cute little round, fat Anglos and put them on our front doorsteps for decorations.

But we won't let the Anglos take care of our kids. We don't need day care and nannies because Mexicans haven't forgotten their families like Anglos have. We take care of each other's kids and we take care of each other. *Como mi primo* Enrique always says, "In Mexico, family is still family. If one person has a job, everybody eats. And everybody takes care of the little ones—*tias y tios, primas y primos, abuelas y abuelos. Todos aman a los ninos.*"

I wrote all that in my essay so I might get an F. It depends on whether McElroy grades it on how well I wrote it, like capital letters and punctuation and good spelling and grammar, or if he grades it on whether he doesn't like my opinion. You never know about teachers. Sometimes they fool you. Like Beecher. She fooled me a lot until I finally figured out that she was smart on a higher level than most people.

I don't care if McElroy gives me a bad grade on my essay. I have to go to summer school anyway because I cut too much before I met Lupe and turned over my new leaf. Even if McElroy flunks my essay, it doesn't matter because I know it's a good essay and I'm glad I wrote it.

# Chapter 10

Today McElroy got in big trouble for letting us talk about God and homosexuals in class except he didn't let us. He just couldn't stop us. I didn't do any talking. But just listening was enough to give me a headache from trying to figure out who was right and who was wrong. We were supposed to be learning how to do analogies but as soon as McElroy said who wants to try number one, T.J. Ritchie said something stupid just to be funny and this kid beside him who is almost as big as T.J. said, "Shut up, you fag," and Curtis Coleman hollered, "Don't be so homophobic!" McElroy tapped his ruler on his desk and said, "That's enough," but T.J. jumped up and said, "Who you calling homophobic?" and Curtis said, "Just about everybody in this pathetic excuse for a town." Curtis is a intellectual who moved here from California last year and he's always talking about how much better it is in California. Usually we don't argue with him because we know he's probably right except sometimes you get tired of somebody reminding you that your hometown sucks.

The kid who called T.J. a fag said, "Don't pee your pants, Curtis. I was just kidding," but Curtis is hard to stop once he starts talking. He said, "Well, it's not funny. People can't help it if they're gay and it's not right to hate them and call them fags." Joey Dinwiddie said, "Oh yes, it is because it says in the Bible you shouldn't be gay or you will burn in hell.

Curtis made this real big sigh and then he said, "If you are referring to the passage in Leviticus that says homosexuality is a sin, then you also know that gluttony and sloth are sins. So that means if you believe gay people are going to burn in hell, everybody who eats like a pig and lives like a slob is going to burn in hell, too. It's going to be a very popular place and a lot of you guys will be there."

McElroy clapped his hands and said, "That's enough," but nobody paid attention to him. He didn't go over and call security, though. He just flopped into his chair and put his head in his hands.

Joey Dinwiddie said, "Yeah, that's enough out of you, Curtis," but Curtis said, "I don't understand why you guys are so interested in other people's sexual preference. It's none of your business—unless you are planning to ask them for a date."

"Because I don't like fags," Joey said. "They make me sick."

McElroy stood up but he didn't have to clap his hands and tell us to be quiet because Henry Dominguez stood up, too, and he said, "Shut up" and the way he said "shut up" made everybody do it. Nobody said anything for a long time and then Henry said, "That's enough" and he sat back down and nobody still said anything because then we all remembered that last year Henry's cousin killed himself after his parents told him they wished he was never born if he was going to be gay.

After Henry's cousin killed himself, a bunch of people wrote letters to the newspaper and said they were sorry to say it but that boy was better off dead. After that, the library put up a little paper on the wall on Gay Pride Week and they put the names of some books you could read if you were gay so you would get some self-esteem and not kill yourself like Henry's cousin did. And the church people made a big protest and now a bunch of church people won't let their kids go to the library anymore which Lupe says is ridiculous.

"They shouldn't be afraid of ideas," Lupe says. "The only people who are afraid of ideas are dumb people who don't know how to think for themselves. Smart people don't believe everything they read. Just because something is in a book doesn't mean it's true."

After McElroy's class, I asked Lupe what did she think about being gay and she said she thinks people are probably gay because of their chromosomes. She's big on biology because she's going to be a doctor. I said, "I don't mean how come people are gay? I mean do you think they are going to hell?" and Lupe said, "I'm not sure there is a hell."

I said, "For real?" and she said, "I'm not even sure there is a God." When she said that, I crossed myself without even planning to. It was automatic. Lupe laughed and said, "Don't worry, Eddie. If there is a God, He isn't going to kill you for wondering if He exists. He'd be glad that you were using the magnificent brain He gave you. And if there isn't a God, then you don't have to worry about wondering."

I asked Lupe wasn't she Catholic and she said yes and I said then how come she could say those kind of things and she said because she doesn't believe anything unless you can prove it. I said nobody can prove there is a God and she said, "Maybe. Maybe not. I'm researching it."

I laughed because how can you research God, but Lupe said she Googled God on the Internet and He has so many hits it will take her years to read them all. She said some of the web sites are just stupid but a lot of them are intellectually stimulating. Like she said there are some historians who say that in the original Bible, God was a man and a woman but, later on, He got changed to just a man. "I ordered a book about it from Amazon.com," Lupe said, "because they wouldn't order it for me at the bookstore here. They said it was blasphemous."

Lupe was impressed that I know what "blasphemous" means, but I learned it last year because a preacher burned a bunch of books right down the street from our house. Before that, I used to go to church with *mi abuela* on Sundays because I figured if I got run over by a bus or something sometime and I hadn't gone to confession, I would still have some good points in my favor for taking a *vieja* to church. But after that preacher burned all the books, I stopped going to church because the whole town knew he was going to do it and they didn't even stop him. He and some of his church friends went to the store and bought a bunch of Harry Potter and Shakespeare books and burned them up. They didn't even read them first. They said they didn't have to read them to know they were full of witchcraft and Satanism. And a whole bunch of other people went and stood by that book burning preacher. They made a holy bonfire. It was in the newspapers and on TV all over the country so now Rosablanca is famous for having crazy book-burners living here.

That book-burning made me so mad for two things. One, I know so many little kids who never even owned one book of their own and if you gave them one, they would wrap it up in a cloth when they weren't reading it so it wouldn't get dusty. And number two, if you burned even one little corner of a page of a book in school, they would expel you for good. I know that for a fact because there was this kid named Corey who lit his math book on fire one day just to show this girl he would do it and they kicked him out of school so fast and wouldn't let him come back because he wouldn't tell them why he did it. They accidentally labeled him an arsonist just like they accidentally labeled me a sex offender except they didn't kick me out of school forever. But the school psychologist said Corey was dangerous and they expelled him for good. So when that preacher burned those books, I thought for sure they would kick him out of the church and make him go be one of those warehouse preachers who has like six people in the audience and they are all family. Maybe they would even arrest him. But they didn't arrest him or even yell at him, and they didn't kick him out of the church. They just let him keep on going around talking about Jesus like they were best friends or something.

That preacher talks too much if you ask me. He should stop talking about going to hell all the time and just go around acting like he is Jesus. Not wearing a white dress and Birkenstocks all the time, but like if he had one of those families in his neighborhood who lives in a falling-down trailer and no electricity and all kinds of junk in the yard, he wouldn't sell his house and move to a nicer neighborhood. He would just go down real quiet to the electric company and pay to have that family's power turned on, and he would take them some bags of real delicious food and not just a cardboard box full of canned beans and peas with dust on the top because people had them in the back of their cupboard for ten years before they donated them to the food bank. Or if he saw that crazy lady who sits outside the library with all her stuff in a bag, he would go over and give her $100 and say a prayer for her and hug her even if she stinks a little bit. And he wouldn't tell anybody he did that stuff. He would just do it nice and quiet. And he would adopt a little orphan from some poor country. Not a movie-star-looking orphan, neither, but a real ugly kid that nobody would want, and he would bring the ugly kid home and feed it good and raise it up right and send it to college so it could be a doctor or a teacher or a judge someday.

And if he saw a gay teenager that nobody liked who always hung out by himself, he wouldn't wish that kid was dead or think about killing him or tell him he is going to burn in hell forever. Even if that gay kid was the preacher's own kid, he wouldn't say he wished the kid had never been born so he would feel like killing himself. He would be nice to that gay kid and he would love that kid even if the kid was against his religion.

Now I know why *mi abuela* won't let people talk about religion when we're eating except to say a prayer at the beginning because everybody would get indigestion from yelling at each other. Everybody has an opinion about God, but nobody can go look it up in the encyclopedia to win the bet and make the other people pay their ten dollars for being so stupid like *mi primo* Enrique always does.

Enrique says you should pretend you believe in God, even if you aren't sure, because if you believe in God and you die and there isn't one, then you were just stupid when you were alive. But if you don't believe in God and then you die and there he is, you're in big trouble. I don't think it would do you any good to just pretend to believe in God because if God is so smart, He would know you were just faking it. But if you said you were sorry, then He would have to forgive you for faking it because that's not a Ten Commandment. But Enrique says, "No way. If God catches you faking it, He'll get real pissed and you'll be sorry." That's why I try not to think about if there is a God because it gives me a headache. I'm just going to wait and see what Lupe finds out.

# Chapter 11

Lupe's father has eyes like a bull fighter, real shiny and hard so you know he could just stand there until the very last second and then stick a knife in your neck right when you thought you were winning. No wonder Lupe is so strong with a father like that. The first time I met Mr. Garcia, he didn't look at me with hard eyes because he didn't hate me yet. But he looked me over real good so I would know I would only get one chance with him so I better not mess it up. But I did. I messed it up big. Now Lupe isn't even allowed to talk to me because I'm a negative influence over her. I'm probably the most negative influence she ever had because nobody else ever made her get arrested before.

If we still had sex ed in school like they used to, probably the whole thing wouldn't have even happened. Primo says they used to teach stuff that you could do besides you-know-what so nobody would get pregnant or get a disease and they used to give out free condoms, too. But now we just have abstinence, so everybody just does what comes naturally. I was willing to take my chances but Lupe wasn't, and it was making me *loco* until Jaime and his girlfriend took too many chances. Then I was glad that Lupe is the boss of us sometimes and makes me listen to her or else.

Jaime bought some birth control pills from T.J. Ritchie except they turned out to be baby aspirins. Lena freaked out and said they had to go to Planned Parenthood right away but Jaime doesn't have a driver's license. His father took it away after Jaime got busted trying to get into a nightclub in El Paso with his father's ID. So Jaime asked me would I take him. Papi already took away my car and sold it and gave me that stupid bicycle that I never ride, so I told Papi I had a job interview right after school and he let me borrow his car. Jaime said to just let him take the car, but I'm not that stupid. I didn't really want to go because I stopped cutting classes and I been trying to bring up my grades so Lupe won't be ashamed of having a dumb boyfriend. But Jaime and me have been friends since first grade and he always has my back, so I had to help him out. We made a plan to cut out right before lunch so we could be back in time for sixth period.

I knew I shouldn't have let Lupe come with us but my brain isn't my biggest body part when she's around, if you know what I mean. When Lupe found out the plan, she said she was going, too, because Lena needed another girl to sit with her. I said no, and she said yes, and I said no, and Lupe put her hands on her hips, and I gave up because when a woman puts her hands on her hips, if you don't give her what she wants, you'll be sorry.

Everything would have been just fine because Lena wasn't pregnant, but I got filled with lust and let Jaime drive back to school so I could sit in the back seat with Lupe. Lena wasn't in the mood to even talk to Jaime, so I figured why waste the back seat on two people who didn't even want to hold hands. Lena cried all the way back to school and it made Jaime so nervous that he crashed the car. We almost made it, but he drove right into the back of a big black SUV about two blocks from the school. This old Anglo guy was driving, so you know he has insurance and he quick called the cops. If it would have been a Mexican car, we could have probably just gave the guy some money because *mi Primo* Octavio can do any kind of body work you need and you can't even tell the car was crashed after he gets done.

Mr. Garcia got there even before the police and as soon as he saw nobody got hurt, he said, "Eduardo, why don't we take a little walk?" It wasn't a real question because he already had his arm around my shoulder. We walked about fifty feet and then Mr. Garcia stopped and said, "Look at my daughter." Lupe was still standing by the smashed up cars talking to the police who was Sgt.Cabrera, that lady cop who came to Beecher's class and I had to be the escort. When the cop car pulled up and I saw who was driving, I was hoping Sgt. Cabrera wouldn't remember me, but as soon as she got out of the car, she said, "Yo, Eddie. How'd you like that book?"

After I escorted her, Sgt. Cabrera sent me that book she was talking about, *The Four Agreements*, except I never read it. I just put it in the back of the little drawer where I keep my socks and forgot about it, but I told her it was real good and thanks for sending it to me.

Sgt. Cabrera shook her head but she didn't call me a liar. Instead, she said, "You don't read that book here," and she pointed to her head. "You read it here." She put her hand on her heart like saying the Pledge of Allegiance. Then she stopped being friendly because she had to arrest me and call my parents.

I was glad Mr. Garcia got there first because other people's parents never yell at you as loud as your own parents do. When I saw his face, I thought Mr. Garcia might punch me, but instead he said let's take a little walk so we did. "Look at my beautiful daughter," he said again. We both looked at Lupe. I nodded because I couldn't say anything because Lupe is so beautiful it can make you cry.

"She's not just beautiful," Mr. Garcia said. "She's gifted and talented, and she is going to make something big out of her life." Usually it's the mothers who say that kind of stuff and usually you think, yeah, right, keep dreaming lady, but Mr. Garcia wasn't dreaming. Lupe is so smart and *hermosa* that she sparkles and her parents are so proud they shine from it, and I am the kind of kid who is so stupid he makes his father almost get a heart attack and makes his mother cross herself and whisper *"Madre de Dios"* about twenty times a day.

"Lupe deserves a man she can respect," Mr. Garcia said, "a man I can respect," and he poked his finger into his chest which must be pretty hard because it sounded like he was knocking on wood. So when Mr. Garcia said he thought it would be a good idea if Lupe didn't see me for a while except in school, I didn't argue with him. Besides, I knew I would probably be grounded forever anyways after Papi got there.

Me and Mr. Garcia were still about twenty feet away, but I could hear Papi yelling on the phone when Sgt. Cabrera called him. I was thinking how embarrassed I would be when he showed up and started yelling at me in front of everybody, but he didn't even yell. He rode up on that stupid bicycle he bought me after he took away my car and just got off the bike and let it fall on the ground. Then he snapped his fingers at me and pointed to the bike, so I knew I wasn't riding home in his car.

When I finally got home, I told Papi I didn't even care if he grounded me forever because it didn't matter anyway since Mr. Garcia said Lupe couldn't go out with me anymore. She can't even call me on the phone because I'm such a negative influence and a loser. Papi said Mr. Garcia is pretty smart because him and Papi are thinking down the same road. He said Jaime and Primo are negative influences over me, so he's sending me to Truth or Consequences to stay with his brother, *mi Tio Antonio,* until school gets out for the summer. Tio is a park ranger and a bachelor and he is totally buff and he's going to whip my *nalgas* into shape. I hope he does it, too, because then maybe Lupe and Papi and everybody can stop being ashamed of me and start being proud of me for a change.

I been to T or C a lot of times to visit, so it's not like I'm going someplace where I don't know my way around or anything. *Mi Primo* Miguel used to live there until he graduated and went to TVI in Albuquerque and got a real good job as an X-ray technician at a hospital which is when my mother made me promise that I would start setting a good example for *los niños* and graduate high school because I'm way smarter than Miguel. So anyways, I been to T or C a lot and the last time I was there, I found this bookstore called The Black Cat downtown near the skateboard park. It's a little bookstore, not like Barnes and Noble or Hastings where if a guy who looks like me goes there right away, the detective starts following him around waiting for him to steal something.

The Black Cat doesn't even have a detective, just this one lady with long yellow hair and a green hat. Not a church hat. Just a hat for fun. When I walked in, she didn't even look nervous like I might steal something. She just said, "Hello," and kept on petting her cat who sneaked down and ate my shoelaces when I was busy looking at the books. The lady even offered to buy me some new laces but it wasn't her fault, and besides it made me feel kind of special for a cat to eat my shoelaces, so I told her never mind.

It was a Saturday when I went to the bookstore and the lady told me if I come back the next day, there will be a poetry reading. She said I could hear some of the local poets do their thing but Papi likes to hit the road early in the morning whenever we visit some place so I didn't get to go. I didn't really want to go to the poetry reading back then because that was before I wrote my poems and I still thought poems were all boring like the ones in school. Now I think maybe it would be kind of interesting.

There's a lot of things I used to think I wouldn't like but it turned out I do, like ballroom dancing and writing poetry. *Mi primo* Enrique says I better watch out or else I'm going to turn into an intellectual and then I'll get my ass kicked all the time. I said what about Harvey Castro. He's the smartest kid in school and nobody kicks his ass. Primo said, "Yeah, but you're not Harvey Castro, you're Eddie Corazon." And I said, "Who is Eddie Corazon?" but Primo thought I was making a joke so he just laughed. But it wasn't a joke. It was a real question, except I don't know the answer.

# Chapter 12

I been thinking that since nobody knows me very good in Truth or Consequences, I could maybe change a little bit. Like I could shave my three chin hairs which probably don't look as cool as I thought they did. And I could tuck in my shirt and not wear a bandana and be a intellectual. I could be Eduardo instead of Eddie and start out getting good grades, so right away, I would be lumped with the kiss-ass kids instead of with the losers. I would probably get beat up a little bit, but I can handle it. Besides, after I graduate, I can be as smart as I want to because after you get out of school, people don't beat you up for being smart. They give you money, instead.

It's a good thing I'm just in a gang with *mi primos* in Rosablanca and not with a real gang because I couldn't just decide to quit hanging with a real gang, I would have to get jumped out and maybe even killed. Jaime's brother Xavier tried to get out of The 10th Street Posse and they beat him down so bad they broke all his teeth and they told him if he went back to school, they would kill him so he had to go get a GED instead. Xavier wanted to get out of the posse because of his girlfriend had a baby and Xavier wanted to be a regular dad and not a gangbanger whose kids would probably be little bangers. I used to think I needed the gang so the drug dealers wouldn't try to make me be their go-boy because I would never be walking by myself where they could get me. But after I met Lupe, I started hanging around with her most of the time, and I started thinking about my future just like Xavier. If they heard me say it, they would kill me for sure but I think maybe if the real gangbangers had somebody to love them real good, they wouldn't need to be in a gang. Even if your mother loves you, maybe it isn't enough, because your mother isn't out there on the streets where you have to deal with all kinds of shit. Maybe you need somebody your own age who can look you eye-to-eye and see you for real and still love you anyways and that person tells you to stop acting like a loser and get some goals for your future. Then you don't need a gang or even a bunch of homies to hang with because you don't feel alone and you are going some place.

These are my new thoughts that I am creating so I can have a new reality where I'm not a loser and a negative influence over Lupe. I got these new thoughts from reading that book Sgt. Cabrera gave me. If I wouldn't have read that book, I wouldn't have decided to be a intellectual because I had two other plans. One was to go out and get a gun and get real drunk and steal a car and drive around with the gun on the dashboard so when the cops pulled me over, I would reach for the gun and they would shoot me dead. That wasn't too good of a plan because then Lupe would be sad forever and what if the cop was Sgt. Cabrera who would feel real bad for killing a kid she gave a book to. My other plan was to take off with Enrique and go to Mexico except there aren't hardly any good jobs there which is why so many people come here and pick chiles for about two cents an hour.

But after I read *The Four Agreements*, I gave up those plans which turned out to be a real good thing. I wasn't even going to read that book because I looked it over a little bit back when Sgt. Cabrera first gave it to me and it looked pretty lame. It's a real skinny book with hardly any big words. You're just supposed to do four things and your life will change: 1) Always do your best. 2) Don't take anything personally. 3) Never make assumptions. 4) Be impeccable with your word. That's the kind of stuff they teach you in kindergarten or first grade except little kids don't know what "assumption" or "impeccable" means so the teachers just say, "Don't go around thinking you know everything and don't tell lies and if somebody calls you a bad name, they're the stupid one." So it didn't seem like a book you would give to somebody and then act like it was a real big deal.

But I had a lot of time on my hands. After I got arrested, Papi took my cell phone so I can't even text anybody and he canceled the Internet, so no email, neither. For a couple days, I had electronics withdrawal. My ears felt so empty that it made a loud echo inside my head and I was wishing that I could go someplace to get away from myself. If I wasn't a secret reader, I probably would have lost it like Jaime's neighbor who married a church girl and then tried to quit drinking and smoking and watching porn all at the same time and it freaked him out so bad he drank some Drano and had to get locked up for his own good. But whenever I felt like I was losing it, I would just read a book.

After I read all the books in the house, I was packing up my stuff to take over to Tio's and I found *The Four Agreements* under my socks. I figured I might as well read it because, even though Sgt. Cabrera was a cop, she was kind of cool and you could tell from looking in her eyes that she was still hanging in there. Sometimes if you look at old people, even if they aren't drunk or stoned, they have this look in their eyes like it's all over so who cares. Maybe they wish they never got married or why did they have that last kid or why couldn't they have normal kids instead of the ones they got and how come they let their wife make them sell their motorcycle or they could be thinking that it's all just a big rip-off because even if you live your life real clean and work hard and save your money and go to church every week and never beat your kids or have adultery, you could still end up with a life that sucks.

As soon as I read that book, I could see why Sgt. Cabrera said you have to read it with your heart and not your head because it sounds too simple to give you any good advice unless you take it to the next level. Like instead of just not telling lies to other people, you shouldn't tell lies to yourself, neither. Like if you really care about graduating high school, then don't tell yourself you don't care and flunk all your classes and then wonder why you're such a loser.

Before, I didn't get it when Sgt. Cabrera said your thoughts create your reality. That sounds like one of those feeling good posters they hang on the wall that nobody reads. But this time, I got it. The light turned on in my brain and it was shining so bright that I could see all my lame ideas just sitting in there looking at me with a stupid expression on their face. Like I saw that thought which was *How long could a girl like Lupe love a loser like me?* And I knew if I kept that thought in my head, Lupe would stop loving me and I would be a loser for real and end up in jail or something.

I used to didn't get the connection because I skipped the middle part about intentions. I was thinking that your thoughts can't create reality because if that worked, then all those losers who think they are going to be NBA superstars or rap masters some day would actually be those things. You can't just think stuff and create a reality, you have to think of an intention to make something happen. Like you can just go around thinking how much you hate school and you still won't be a juvenile delinquent unless you make an intention to get in trouble like I did, so I ended up at the alt school. And I created the intention to get a girlfriend so I joined ballroom dance and got Lupe and now we got our own reality. Then I created the stupid intention to lie to Papi about his car and I created everybody getting arrested.

So I kicked all the old thoughts out of my head to make room for a bunch of new ones with good intentions attached to them. Now I don't even think of letting go of Lupe or being a loser. Instead I am creating the thought of being a success and making the intention to graduate and get a good job and maybe even go to college so I can be the kind of man who can look Lupe's father straight in the eye for as long as it takes.

The reason I'm thinking on maybe going to college is this dude from New Mexico State came to McElroy's class to inspire us to go to college and he was a professor, even though he was Mexican and had a moustache and a pony tail. After he got done inspiring us and everybody was fooling around, I asked that professor what if somebody's grades were real good for a few years and then real bad for some more years and then real good right at the end. He said as long as your senior year is real good, you can probably go to NMSU if you graduate and get some good recommendations from your teachers. McElroy might give me a good recommendation because he would be happy that he was a good influence and I didn't drop out of school, but I don't want to ask him. He probably doesn't even know all the stuff I been thinking, but it's not right to ask somebody to do you a favor after you been going around thinking they are a stupid *pinche* dickhead.

Beecher would probably give me a recommendation if I asked her, unless she already forgot who I am. She's still working at the library so I guess she didn't go teach those Indian kids like I thought she would. She probably wants to wait until next year so she can start fresh instead of taking over for some crappy teacher that got fired or just quit because it was too hard trying to motivate people like me and Henry Dominguez and T.J. Ritchie.

At first, I was thinking that maybe I would check out some library books sometime when Beecher wasn't working and then the next time I went to pick up Letty and the boys from story hour, I would put the books in that book drop and I would put my journal in there, too. If some other library lady got it, she would probably just throw my journal away since it doesn't have my name on it or anything. But if Beecher got it, she might recognize how I write. She might even remember some of the other stuff I wrote. Like this one essay she gave me extra credit for having a sense of humor. Beecher would give you a better grade for having a sense of humor, even if you used a swear word or bad spelling because she liked us to have our own ideas.

"You can always correct the spelling and grammar in an interesting essay," Beecher used to tell us, "but if your essay is perfect and boring, then it's perfectly boring." Before they killed Saddam Hussein, Beecher asked us to write in our journal what we thought Saddam would be like if he was a kid in our class at Bright Horizons. And here's what I wrote:

> Well, let me tell you. If Saddam Hussein was a kid in this class today we wouldn't have all this war stuff and lot of people wouldn't be dying. Also if he was a kid in this class we wouldn't make all those diaper on your head jokes because we aren't allowed to hurt people's feelings. Saddam would probably have a dad who owned a Pik Quik and he would get all the sodas he wanted. Or else his dad might own a gas station and he would get free gas so everybody would be his friend. And if he was in this class today, I think Saddam would probably wear some cheap plastic shoes and those polyester slacks with a plaid button-up shirt and once in a while he would wear some bellbottoms. Or else he would wear camouflage clothes because he likes to look like he's in the army. He would probably wear sideburns because he would think they were cool except he wouldn't comb his hair or brush his teeth and never clean his ears so he would

*have real yellow teeth and his ears would be full
of that earwax junk. Probably his feet would smell
like Nacho Cheese Doritos. Nobody would want
to sit next to him and then Miss Beecher would
say, "Everybody sit in the first four rows except
Saddam you can sit in the back." If somebody did
sit behind him they would stick him with their
pencil.*

*Saddam would have terrible social skills. He would
steal people's lunch money and he would always
write dirty stuff on the desks so even Miss Beecher
wouldn't like him. When nobody was looking,
she would hit him in the head. For sure, Saddam
would always want to copy off everybody but
nobody would let him copy their papers because
he's a punk-ass trick. And if he ever tried to mess
with me, I would beat his ass.*

Beecher gave me a good grade on that journal and she
wrote on the side of the paper, "Watch out for stereotypes,
but thank you for making me smile, Eddie," so maybe she
would remember that smile. But it could be that she forgot
all about me as soon as she stopped being my teacher. Just
because you remember somebody real good doesn't mean
they remember you back.

Before, I was thinking I would put my journal in the
library drop box so Beecher could read all those serious
pages that I wrote and never turned in for a grade because I
didn't want her to know too much personal stuff about me.
And I'd put one of my poems on the last page. But my new
intention is different. Instead of putting it in the drop box,
I will walk right up and hand my journal to Beecher and if
she says, "What's this?" I'll say, "I'm Eddie Corazon in case
you forgot me and that's my journal that I wrote when you
were our teacher but I never gave it to you." And then I'll

say, "I just want you to know that even if you were only there for a couple of months, you were still the best teacher I ever had." And then I will probably start feeling weird and I will feel like running right out of the library but I won't run. I will stand right there and wait.

# Chapter 13

It worked. I created my new reality in Truth or Consequences. Everybody calls me Eduardo and I sit with the brains and brownies at school. I wasn't sure I would like being a intellectual as much as being a juvenile delinquent, but then I had to think about it with an impeccable attitude. I asked myself straight up which was better and I had to admit it's easier just letting your brain breathe like it wants to instead of always thinking about how you have to be so cool and look ruthless and walk dangerous and pretend you can't hardly even read.

Tio Antonio moved since the last time we visited him. Instead of living in T or C, now he lives in a little brown house at the end of this little park down along the Rio Grande that is part of Elephant Butte State Park. It's way different from living in a town. Mostly it is just trees and cactus and a lot of ducks. There are about ten little adobe *casitas* where people can camp and a walking trail that goes all along the river so you can stop and fish or have a picnic. There isn't any school out there, so I ride the bus to T or C which has a brand new high school that looks a lot better than most schools in New Mexico which usually have so much graffiti and broken stuff they look like Pancho Villa used to hide out there.

Primo was wrong about intellectuals getting their ass kicked all the time. Nobody even tried to mess with me and I'm surrounded by girls because mostly the smart kids are all girls. None of them are as smart as Lupe, though. She writes me a letter every day and I write her one back and then we mail them on Friday so we can read one letter every day until we get the next envelope, but I always read them all at once. And I read them all over again every day, too. Lupe writes just as good as the people who write our books in school, so I always make sure I spell everything right and use my good grammar so she'll know I'm not a *menso*. At first, I kept Lupe's letters under my pillow, but pretty soon there were so many it was making my neck hurt so I stuck them under my mattress for sweet dreams.

I don't have to stick Lupe's letters under the mattress to hide them from Tio because he doesn't even snoop in my room. He trusts me. Like he told me I couldn't use the Internet to send any emails, just to surf the Internet for school projects or else read the news. I figured he would check up on me, but he hardly even uses his computer. I thought about sneaking one little email to Lupe but I didn't do it because Mr. G looks like the kind of father who would say he trusts you but he would still check up on you just in case and if he saw my email, then he would know I'm a sneaky liar and not the kind of man he can respect. Plus, I gave Tio my word of honor and I wouldn't break it even if I didn't care about Mr. G.

Every day, I have to come straight home from school and help Tio who is already home because he starts work at five-o'clock in the morning. Tio doesn't sit around after work and watch TV sports or hang out in the bar like a normal bachelor. He does projects. Hard projects that make you sweat, like building a cement block wall or hauling a bunch of 8x8's down to the river and digging up some dirt so we can put them along the trail to make a nice border. Tio doesn't eat like a normal bachelor, neither. Instead of burritos and cheeseburgers and beers, he eats organic brown rice and vegetables and when he makes a barbecue, he fires up some salmon steaks instead of real steaks. He drinks iced tea that smells funny, a little bit like old socks, but it doesn't taste too bad and it makes you feel calm and smooth inside because it's herbalized and doesn't have caffeine which is a artificial stimulant. I thought I would get even skinnier eating this kind of food, but I'm getting thicker in some places. It must be all that work Tio makes me do and no sodas or chips to be found in this whole house because I checked.

Tio won't let me watch regular TV, neither, just PBS or BBC. Not for a punishment, though. More like for principles. Tio has more principles than anybody I ever knew. He says TV rots your brain and the commercials make you think you need stuff you don't need because you wouldn't even know that stuff existed if you didn't see it on TV so how could you need it. Plus he says there's enough violence in the world already without making up more for the TV addicts. I was pretty surprised but after only about two days, I stopped missing TV. I like it better to just walk down by the river and think. Sometimes I sit on one of the picnic tables under the trees and read a book or write a poem for Lupe or sometimes just sit and let my brain float down the river like a fat lazy duck. At first, the river was real low and sad-looking and the coyotes could walk right out in the middle and catch a fish which I saw with my own eyes one day, but pretty soon the rains started up in the mountains and then they opened up the dam so the ranchers could irrigate and now the Rio Grande really looks like a river somebody would sing a song about.

One day I got up when Tio did, just to see how it feels to be awake that early and then he left for work and I went outside because I never saw a sunrise before when I was sober. Now I know what people are talking about when they say the light in New Mexico is different from any place else so all the artists like to move here. Even though I never been to another state, I could tell the light was special because the whole world turned kind of yellow with pink around the edges. Then I saw this bird that was bigger than any bird I ever saw with a real long neck and a black ring around its eye. It flew right over my head and I could hear the wings flapping so loud it sounded like they were hydraulic. If you never saw a big bird in a real quiet place, then you don't know they make all that noise when they fly around, kind of like if you see one of those programs on PBS where the ballerinas are dancing, if you turn off the sound, they look light and fluffy but if you turn up the sound, they sound like an elephant stomping around. That bird was a blue heron. I looked it up in one of Tio's books. He has about a thousand books, mostly about animals and places you can go camping and backpacking where you have to bring everything yourself including toilet paper and a little shovel to dig a toilet pit and you have to watch out for bears and mountain lions.

When I asked Tio wasn't he afraid to go some place where a mountain lion might chew off his leg, he said he would take his chances against a mountain lion any day instead of a punk with a gun in his hand and a head full of hate. Tio talks like that sometimes, like a poem. Beecher would probably like him. Lots of women like him. I can tell by the way they look at him when we go to a store or something, but he doesn't have a girlfriend and he never got married. For a while, I was wondering was he gay and I decided even if he was, it didn't matter because he wasn't a pervert who would do something bad to me, but then one morning I woke up and I saw this real fine lady tiptoeing outside to her car and Tio standing at the window drinking his stinky herbalized tea and watching her go.

Keeping my word of honor about not sending emails turned out real good because yesterday Tio said I could email Lupe because I been doing so good in school that my new English teacher called up my parents and told them I'm an excellent student and a good example for the other kids which is what you would call irony if it was in your literature book. When Papi called me up and said he got a call from one of my teachers, I started to feel like I was going to throw up all that brown rice that Tio's been feeding me. But then he said, "Your mother is so proud of you, son," and I knew he meant he was, too, except he isn't too good at saying that kind of stuff. I'm not, neither. Like I never thanked him for being a good dad who cares about his kids. So I told him thanks for sending me to stay with Tio where I could get rehabilitated and not turn into an incorrigible juvenile delinquent who is a shame to the whole family.

Living with Tio is interesting, even if it isn't too normal. Like on this one weekend, he took me to this bath house in T or C downtown in a real old kind of crumbly place where the bath part looked like those real old showers they have at the gym where they look dirty even if you scrub them every day, but Tio said don't worry there's no germs because of the water is 115 degrees right out of the ground. That water is supposed to have some kind of miracle minerals that heal you if you got achy bones or some kind of sickness that the doctors don't know. The whole downtown of T or C has way hot water under it, so if you live down there, you can go out in your back yard and dig a well and have your own personal hot tub.

Inside the bath house, we went to the men's section where there were five bathtubs made all out of tile with real big faucets. You could close a long curtain in front of your bathtub so you could take off all your clothes and nobody could see you unless they drilled a little hole in the wall to peek through like they do in those creepy motels. There was a little hole in the wall between my bathtub and the next bathtub, so I hung my towel over the hole. It's a good thing they had a cold water faucet on that bathtub because that water was H-O-T *caliente*. It shriveled me up and turned me red and wrinkled like a little baby, but after a couple minutes I started to like it. I laid back in the water and floated like an old stick and pretty soon I felt my brain start floating, too. I got the same feeling I get when Lupe kisses me real soft like a feather.

After ten minutes, Tio knocked on my curtain and said I had to get out of the water because it was my first time. Besides, we had to take a shower and get dressed because Tio was going to drop me off at The Black Cat so I could hear the poetry reading while he went grocery shopping and changed the oil in his truck. I would of chickened out from going to the poetry reading except when I told Tio I might go there sometime, he offered to drop me off and I didn't want to look like a little kid afraid to do something just because he never did it before.

There was a sign on the door of the bookstore that said, *Welcome to Coffee and Confusion: Open Mic.* At first, I was kind of nervous to go in there because there weren't any other kids, just old people and most of them pretty white. But then, I saw that a bunch of the old men had pony tails and a couple people looked like they could even be Mexican. So I went and stood inside the door and I heard this one old hippy-looking dude in a black baseball cap talking to this lady with white hair who looked like a grandmother except the dude said, "The lemmings don't give a shit because they don't know shit, and then they get in your shit and talk shit about you," and the lady didn't scream or tell him to clean up his language. She just laughed. Then the owner of the bookstore with the long yellow hair saw me and waved at me and pointed to a chair in the corner. So I sat down and waited.

Pretty soon this real skinny old dude with a little white goatee got up and started reading a poem about some black dude beating him up when he was in school and after that they got to be friends. Then another old guy with purple hair got up and read a poem about doesn't it break your heart to live in a country that is a country apart from the rest of the world because of the war in Iraq, and everybody clapped a lot. Then this lady with pink glasses and wearing a long skirt but a man's shirt got up and played her guitar and made everybody sing "I wanna go home" every couple of seconds. After that, a real short lady from Iran read this poem about how home isn't where you live, it's where you love. She first read the poem in her own language and even though I couldn't understand it, I could tell it sounded better before she turned it into English. Just like when you have a song in Spanish where the words say, "I'm a sincere man from the land of the palm trees and before I die, I want to share the poetry in my soul. My poetry is clear green and burning red, my poetry is a wounded deer that you seek in the forest," when they translate it to English they say, "I write my songs with no learning, and yet with truth they are burning," just to make a rhyme out of it.

After that, about fifteen more people read their poems and stories. It was sort of weird but it was nice to be sitting in a place where everybody was laughing and feeling happy about listening to each other read and nobody making fun of each other, even if the stuff they wrote wasn't too good or they had a squeaking voice or made a mistake and had to read something over twice.

Right at the end, the skinny guy with the beard got up and said, "We have a new reader this week. Her name is Ramona and she just moved here from North Carolina. Let's give her a warm welcome." Everybody clapped real polite and this lady went up to the front. She had short brown hair, not flat and shiny but sticking up all over the place like little chocolate curls. She said, "I have never read in front of an audience before, so please excuse me if I blush." You could tell she was nervous because her face looked like she just ate a *habanero chile* but the rest of her was the same color as a peach. She talked with a big Southern accent like I never heard except in the movies. And she read this story she wrote about how books changed her life. I even remember part of it. She said, "I just love books. I love everything about them, the way they look and smell and feel. And sometimes, when I'm fixin' to start reading a new book, I sit and hold it in my hands a while and think about it, the way some folks sit and ponder their travel brochures. And when I open a new book, I always hope that the words will capture me and carry me off to some new place and that when I get there, I will be far, far away from me."

I knew exactly what she meant which was weird because there she was, this kind of old Anglo lady from thousands of miles away with a whole different kind of life from me, but she told a story that could have came out of my own mouth.

# Chapter 14

Last Sunday, there was another poetry reading at the Black Cat and Tio didn't even ask me if I wanted to go. He just said what time does it start and was I going to read any of my poems. Tio is the only person except Lupe who ever read my poems. He said he doesn't know diddly-squat about poetry but he thought they were pretty good. Diddly-squat is the kind of thing Tio gets from working around too many Anglos and he thinks it's real funny to copy their accent. He's always saying things like "get her done" and "well, I'll be danged."

I don't even get nervous going to the Black Cat anymore because I went there a couple of times just to look around, and one day when there wasn't anybody else in there, that lady with the yellow hair told me her name was Rhonda and she asked me did I want some coffee because it was on the house since she was going to empty out the coffee pot pretty soon. I took the coffee because I didn't want to hurt her feelings after she told me her name and everything, but I had to dump it out in the bathroom because it tasted so bad. I never drank coffee before. It smells kind of good but it's one of those things like vanilla or whisky that if you drink it straight, you'll be sorry.

I took one of my poems to the reading, but I didn't sign up my name to read. I couldn't stand there in front of all those people and read something so personal. I been thinking maybe I would write something about the river or that blue heron or something that wasn't about me so maybe I could read it. That North Carolina lady, Ramona, was there again and I sat in the chair next to her except I didn't say

84

anything, just sat there and smelled her perfume which smelled exactly like Lupe so I felt happy and sad both at the same time. Ramona read another story about this girl who was seventeen and went to visit her brother who was in the navy. The girl decided she was tired of being a virgin so she spent the whole night with a sailor who thought she was beautiful. When her brother found out, he said he would kill that guy and he choked his sister and then he started crying. Even though it was a pretty sad story, Ramona told it real funny and everybody laughed so loud.

The next weekend after that, Tio and me drove over to Rosablanca to visit my family. Even though it's only a couple months since I saw them, they looked different, especially my parents. They didn't used to have wrinkles or gray hairs. Letty and the boys kept hanging on my arms and legs and asking me did I want to play a game or they showed me all the junky stuff they made in art class in school. I told them to stop because they gave me a pain in the ass but they probably knew I was just saying that stuff so I wouldn't feel like crying because they just laughed and didn't let go.

Tio let me borrow his truck and Mr. G let me drive Lupe over to Caliches for a frozen custard. At first, I felt kind of shy but as soon as we got around the corner from her house, Lupe hollered, "Pull over. Quick!" so I hit the brakes. As soon as we pulled to the curb, Lupe jumped in my lap and kissed me all over my face and neck and ears. I told her she scared me and I thought it was a real emergency and she said, "You don't think this is an emergency?" and kissed me some more until it was a real emergency and we had to go get that custard to cool us down.

After we ate our custard, Lupe wiped her mouth real careful with a napkin and then she leaned over and put her hands on my face and I thought she was going to kiss me except she said, "Eddie, I have to tell you something and it's real bad." For a second, my brain started yelling "pregnant!" but that couldn't happen unless Lupe was messing around on me and I knew she wasn't, so then I started thinking maybe she got a new boyfriend while I was gone, but she said, "Primo got busted."

"Which Primo?" I said, except I knew she would say Enrique. He got busted for stealing car stereos and selling them which isn't like a major crime, but he already got busted twice before for some other stuff and once when he got caught shoplifting, he had a gun stuck in his sock. He was a little kid back then so he didn't do any time, but once you got a weapon on your record, the cops watch out for you to grow up and then they get you if you keep on engaging in criminal activities. I told Primo he should go to TVI like Miguel did and get a job in electronics like they show on the commercials but he said he already wasted too much of his life in school and why anybody would go to school if they didn't have to, especially if they had to pay money to go.

"Sorry, Eddie," Lupe said. And I thought she would say something like she usually says, like Primo has the same options as everybody else, but he always take the easy way, the short cuts, because he's in too big of a hurry to stop and think about what he's doing and he thinks he's so slick that he'll never get busted even after he just got busted. But Lupe didn't say anything. She didn't start crying or try to cheer me up or try to pretend like it was no big deal. She just sat there and let things be quiet, which is one of the best things about her. She knows when to shut up and she can shut up for a real long time, too, and not get mad about it after.

When I dropped Lupe off at her house, she kissed me on the nose and said, "*Ay te watcho,*" and jumped out of the truck. I hollered out the window that most girls would probably cry if their boyfriend got sent way over the mountains where she couldn't see him. Lupe came around to the driver's side and stuck her head inside the window and said even if she couldn't see me, she could hear my heart beating at night when she put her head on her pillow. "Besides," she said, "how could I be sad when every time I see you, you're like a new version of my old boyfriend except you get better every time?" Then she walked into her house and didn't even turn around, just swished her *nalgas* back and forth to say *hasta luego.*

When I was over in Rosablanca, I took my journal to the library, too. I walked right in the front door and up to the desk and said could I please speak to Miss Beecher and when she came out, I handed my journal to her just like I planned in my intention. I didn't have to remind her my name, though, because as soon as Beecher saw me, she said, "Hello, Eddie." She started to open my journal but I asked her would she please read it later when I wasn't standing there feeling so nervous. She closed it right away and sort of wrapped her arms around it like a hug. Then I told her how I was thinking on going to college but I would need a good recommendation from a teacher, so could she please consider writing one for me. Then I started thinking maybe she would think I said she was the best teacher I ever had just so she would write me a recommendation.

"Even if you don't want to recommend me, I still meant what I said about you being the best teacher," I told her.

"I know you aren't a manipulative person, Eddie," Beecher said. "And I would be delighted to write you a recommendation. I hope you go to college and earn your Ph.D. in English so you can be a literature professor some day. Unless you'd rather be a high school teacher because you like high school so much." Then she laughed out loud for a minute until she remembered we were at the library so she put her hand over her mouth and kept on laughing so her hair shook all around her face with little shivers like it was laughing too.

I know Beecher was just joking about me being a teacher, but all the way driving back to T or C, I kept remembering what she said and having a little picture in my mind of me being a teacher. I would let people write whatever they wanted to, just like Beecher did, and if they said they didn't care if they graduated, I would make them read *The Four Agreements* so they could learn how to think impeccable thoughts. I don't think I would ever be a teacher, but a lot of things have happened lately that I never would have believed if you told me they were going to happen, so I'm not making any promises to myself. Except I did make one kind of promise, though. I decided that I'm never going to jail unless it's one of those situations where the cops bust you just for being the wrong color in the wrong place at the wrong time.

I had so many things to think about after that visit and I had a lot of time to think on the way back because Tio likes to listen to music while he's driving, so he doesn't care if you don't talk to him. He was listening to this cassette he bought off a guy who works at Mail Boxes Etc who is in this band called *Caliente!* The music was pretty good so we didn't say anything all the way across 70 East from Alamogordo past White Sands and almost to Cruces. Right when we started to go through that pass where the Organ Mountains start to look real sharp and pretty, Tio turned down the music and said, "You know, Eddie, it's okay if you're still a virgin."

At first, I thought I was tripping because why would Tio say something like that when we never even said one word about sex in the whole time I been at his house. He could have figured it out from reading me and Lupe's letters, but I knew he didn't read them. I was going to say, "What makes you think I'm a virgin?" but I didn't want to hear the answer so I didn't say anything. Then Tio said, "Sorry if I stepped on your toes there, Bud. Just wanted you to know you aren't the Lone Ranger even if you think you are. Most of the guys your age who brag about all the pussy they're getting aren't getting any or they would keep their mouths shut so other guys won't go after their women."

I still didn't know what to say. Me and Lupe got real close a couple times, but we never had official sex because she's Catholic so she couldn't have an abortion and if she had a baby and we got married, then she would end up hating me after she got tired of getting up in the middle of the night to feed a baby who was crying when she should have been in college learning how to be the doctor who delivers the babies.

Tio probably figured he was right since I didn't say anything because he said, "Take your time, *M'ijo*. Take your time." He played a little drums on the steering wheel, then he turned down the music even lower. "I know you think you and Lupe will love each other for the rest of your life and maybe you will. But your hormones are in control right now, so you could start confusing lust and love. Not that you can't have both, but at your age, lust takes priority." He sounded just like Beecher when he said that. I started thinking maybe I should introduce them because Beecher is the only lady I know who is as smart as Tio and she eats the same kind of weird healthy food like he did and I bet she doesn't watch TV, neither.

"Don't worry," I told Tio. "Me and Lupe aren't taking any chances, if that's what you're worried about."

"Lupe reminds me of your mother, you know," Tio said which made me wonder if maybe he drank some beers out back with Papi before we left. "Your mother was the smartest girl in the whole school. Did you know that? Sharp as a razor blade. When she started dating your father, I was so jealous. I wished I had found her first. She was so hot she sizzled." Tio licked his finger and stuck it on his leg and made a fat-in-the-fire sound. "She could have gone to college. She could have been the first woman President. She could have done anything, but she married your dad and then you came along and then Letty and the boys."

I didn't say anything because I was still trying to picture my mother as a hot-babe genius instead of a old lady in a hair net dishing up macaronis and *queso* for little kids in the school cafeteria or roasting chiles in the kitchen at home, but Tio probably thought he hurt my feelings because he quick looked over at me and said, "Hey. She loves you. I'm not saying she's not happy. But I always wonder if she might have been even happier if she had the chance to fly as high as her wings could have taken her."

And I started thinking of all the times I would come into the house and my mother would be standing in the living room staring at the television except it wasn't turned on, or else she would be standing in the middle of the kitchen not even cooking and if I asked her what was she thinking, she would jump a little bit like I scared her and I would have to ask her again and she would say, "Oh, nothing." And I wondered if maybe she had been thinking that her life was nothing, except her life isn't nothing because if it wasn't for her, I would have been a pretty bad criminal or at least dropped out of school and my father would have probably had to go to jail for losing his temper and making a fight with the wrong guy. But maybe saving a couple of loser men and cooking the best *chile rellenos* in the neighborhood doesn't feel like something so big to a woman with a brain as sharp as a razor blade.

That's when I decided not to ask Lupe to marry me until I'm 21 and a big success, or at least a medium-size one. I made the intention to keep on loving Lupe but not hold her back even one little bit. I'll try to go to college with her but if she gets a scholarship to some big fancy school, I will tell her go ahead and be a doctor and open her wings and fly. And I'll go to NMSU and I'll keep writing her one letter a day and I'll write her a bunch of poems, too, enough to make a whole book. And I'll get a good job and make a real nice house so after Lupe is done flying, she'll have a place to make a nest if she wants to. Who knows—I might even do a little bit of flying myself.

# Chapter 15

One more week and school will be over, and I'll go back to Rosablanca and my old life. I started to think what if as soon as I get back there, I start messing up again and go back to being a loser. But Lupe says the real losers are the people who are too afraid to try and see what they can be. So I'm going to try real hard, even though there are some advantages to being a juvenile delinquent—like most of the teachers don't call on you because they don't expect you to know anything, and some really hot girls like bad-ass guys— but you always have to watch your back 24-7. And even though you get a rush from doing stuff like just walking up on the street and asking some old Anglo guy what time is it and he gives you his watch because he thinks you'll kill him or something, you get a different kind of rush from having people clap real loud and whistle when you read a poem that you wrote. And when somebody walks up to you after and says, "Dude, that was so hot you're smokin'," it feels pretty good even if the guy is a old hippie with a white pony tail and a tie-dye t-shirt. And who could complain about having a bunch of grown-up ladies tell you that you're handsome and charming, and they aren't even your family.

Ramona even asked me did I want to join a writer's group where her and some other people meet at the Black Cat and share the stuff they are writing and tell each other what sucks and what's good, but I'm not sure I could do that. It might feel too weird to let people read my poems before they're done and what if I couldn't write any more good ones? But sometimes it's good to do things that feel weird because after you do them a little bit, they feel all right like if you have to wear hard shoes for a wedding or something at first, you miss your tennis shoes but after a while you forget about your feet and you can dance better because those hard shoes are more slippery plus if you got a killer suit to wear, you could wreck the whole thing and look so lame if you wore some old dirty sneakers. So if I lived here, I probably would try to be in the writer's group and see if it started to feel normal after a while except it would probably still feel weird if I told some old person that their poems sucked. I wouldn't say sucked, I would say they stunk or something nice like that, but it would still be weird because they're an old person and you're supposed to respect them if you can. But I couldn't join that group anyway because I'm going back to Rosablanca which is where I belong at least for right now.

I almost wish I could stay in T or C, even though I miss Lupe and Jaime and my family because I got used to writing a letter to Lupe every day and getting a letter from her everyday, too. And I got used to how quiet it is with no TV so you have to go outside and appreciate nature instead.

Some days when I walk by the river, I get a feeling like I *am* the river, *El Rio Eduardo*, and I flow from here to *Méjico*, full of fish and broken sticks and ducks and plastic bags and soda cans that the tourists throw into me because their brains are on vacation, too. I'm going to miss the river and that blue heron and even the weird food that I got used to. Tio taught me how to cook a couple things like brown rice and stir-fry vegetables so I can make the same food like he does. He bought me a wok for a going away present. I bet I'll be the only Mexican kid in town who has his own wok. I can even eat with chopsticks, too, and now I know why Jenny Chu is so skinny.

I'll miss going to the Black Cat, too, and talking to Rhonda and letting Mr. Poe eat my shoelaces. But I'm going to keep working on my poems so when I come visit Tio, I'll have something real good to read. I need some real good poems because now I got a new reputation to maintain. Last Sunday, I got up way early in the morning and went down to the river and wrote a poem in my new journal that Tio bought me for another going-away present. I thought it was a pretty good poem so I took it to the Black Cat, except I chickened out and didn't sign up to read. I just sat there holding my journal with my poems in it, thinking that maybe next year I would come back and read something. But all of a sudden, the guy with the goatee said, "We have a new reader this week and his name is Eddie Corazon. So please give him a warm welcome."

Everybody started clapping and looking at me and I felt like running out the door, but I was sitting too far away and there were so many people I would have to jump over them or step on their feet. Ramona was sitting beside me and she put her hand on my arm and said, "Don't be mad, but I signed you up, Honey Bun." She touched my journal. "I could just feel whatever you got written in that there little book is burning up the pages, trying to get out into the world." Then she stood up and held out her hand and after a couple seconds, I took it and she walked me up to the front and leaned over and kissed me on the cheek. "That's for good luck." When Ramona kissed me, this old guy named Gino who wears a hat like Columbo hollered, "I need some good luck, too!" and took off his hat and put it over his heart.

"Let's hear it, kid," Gino said and everybody got real quiet. It's a good thing I had my journal because my hands were shaking so much that if I had my poem on a piece of paper, it would have rattled so loud nobody could hear me. My journal shook a little bit but it didn't make any noise so my voice came out real loud and it didn't squeak even once like it always used to do which is why I never read out loud in school. While I was reading my poem, in the back of my mind I was surprised because my voice sounded real deep and low, just the way my father sounds.

My poem is mostly English with a little Spanish mixed in to spice it up, and it has a bilingual title: "Veinte-Veinte Vision" which means "20-20 Vision" in case you only know English. Well, here goes:

### VEINTE-VEINTE VISION

*If you don't like your life
you can open a book and follow the words
to some new place
far away from you where you can forget
that you are your father's heart attack
and your mother's tears
and you walk with your eyes looking in
so you won't see yourself in the mirror
because you're afraid to look out el mundo
in case there's no place for you in it*

*Or if you don't like your life
you could create your own book
and follow your own words to some new place
where you write yourself a new life
that makes your parents so proud they shine
when they call you Mi'jo
and you walk with your eyes looking out
so you can see yourself con ojos abierto y claro
and you aren't afraid to look out at the world
because you made your own place in it*

*and even if the book of your life
is a regular everyday story
and not a big bestselling estrella
you will still be glad you wrote every word
with your own mind from your own corazon
in your own blood*

When I finished reading my poem, the old hippy with the white pony tail stood up and whistled, and everybody clapped and clapped so loud that my ears are still full of that noise, like the sound of a blue heron flying right up past your head into the sunrise until it is so high you can't hear it anymore. You just see it floating in the air like a giant grey feather while *el sol* smiles down on the cactus-covered banks of the *Rio Grande* and makes *todo el mundo* shine like gold.

*Ay te watcho.*

# About the Author

LouAnne Johnson started writing stories and poems when she was just a little girl. Here's a picture of her when she was in kindergarten.

When she was 10 years old, LouAnne decided to write books when she grew up. People teased her and said she would never get anything published because it was too hard to write books. But LouAnne kept on writing, even when other people teased her, because her mother had taught her to follow her heart.

"If you really really want to accomplish something," her mother always said, "you have to work really hard and believe in yourself."

So, LouAnne kept on writing. She wrote and wrote and wrote for 18 years until her book, *Making Waves*, was published. Since then, LouAnne has written ten books and all of them have been published!

"Work hard and follow your dreams," LouAnne tells young people. "Don't worry about what other people think. Think for yourself and dream big. Even if your dream doesn't turn out exactly the way you planned it, you will still end up taking a journey that will change your life."

To honor her mother Alyce Shirley, who died from breast cancer in 1999, LouAnne created the name ALYCE SHIRLEYDAUGHTER.

During her life, Alyce Shirley wished people would call her Alyce, but the family insisted on calling her Shirley to avoid confusion because she had an aunt named Alyce.

"I was the only person who called my mother Alyce," LouAnne says, "and after she died, I decided to use the name Alyce Shirleydaughter because I am Alyce Shirley's daughter. I think that name would make my mother smile and she had a beautiful smile."

"I like to imagine my mother perched on the edge of a cloud in the turquoise New Mexico sky, chuckling as she reads the latest Alyce Shirleydaughter book," says LouAnne.

At least 25% of the royalties from every Alyce Shirleydaughter book goes directly to support breast cancer prevention.

**Visit www.alyceshirleydaughter.com
for more information.**

# Books by Alyce Shirleydaughter:

- *What Happened to the Man I Married?*
- *Alternative Ed*
- *Yo! Eddie!*
(the G-rated version of *Alternative Ed*)
- *Vigilante Grandmas*

# Books by LouAnne Johnson:

- *Teaching Outside the Box: how to grab your students by their brains*
- *The Queen of Education*
- *School is Not a Four-Letter Word*
- *Dangerous Minds*
(initially titled *My Posse Don't Do Homework*)
- *The Girls in the Back of the Class*
- *Making Waves: a woman in this man's navy*

Visit these websites for more information, author bio, and photos:

**www.alyceshirleydaughter.com**
**www.louannejohnson.com**